THE HOMECOMING

Connie Shelton

THE BEN PECOS MYSTERY SERIES

by Susan Slater:
The Pumpkin Seed Massacre
Yellow Lies
Thunderbird
Firedancer
Under A Mulberry Moon
The Thaw
Ghost Dust
Paper Arrows
Snake Eyes
A Way to the Manger (a Christmas novella)

by Connie Shelton:
The Homecoming

ALSO BY CONNIE SHELTON

The Charlie Parker Mystery Series
The Samantha Sweet Coxy Bakery Series
The Heist Ladies Caper Mysteries
The Ghost in the Library Mystery Series

THE HOMECOMING

Ben Pecos Mysteries, Book 10

Connie Shelton

Secret Staircase Books

The Homecoming
Published by Secret Staircase Books, an imprint of
Columbine Publishing Group, LLC
PO Box 416, Angel Fire, NM 87710

Copyright © 2025 Connie Shelton
All rights reserved. No part of this book may be reproduced or transmitted in any form or by any means, electronic or mechanical, including photocopying, recording, or by an information storage and retrieval system without permission in writing from the publisher. No portion of this book may be used for the training of any artificial intelligence (AI) model without express written permission from the publisher and compensation paid to the author.
This book is a work of fiction. Names, characters, places and incidents are either the product of the author's imagination or are used fictitiously. Any resemblance to actual events or locales or persons, living or dead, is entirely coincidental. Although the author and publisher have made every effort to ensure the accuracy and completeness of information contained in this book we assume no responsibility for errors, inaccuracies, omissions, or any inconsistency herein. Any slights of people, places or organizations are unintentional.

Book layout and design by Secret Staircase Books
Cover images © Meunierd, Yulia Lelekova, Evgenii Naumov
First trade paperback edition: November, 2025
First e-book edition: November, 2025

* * *

Publisher's Cataloging-in-Publication Data

Shelton, Connie
The Homecoming / by Connie Shelton.
p. cm.
ISBN 978-1649142290 (paperback)
ISBN 978-1649142306 (e-book)

1. Ben Pecos (Fictitious character)—Fiction. 2. New Mexico—Fiction. 3. Pueblo Indian tribes—Fiction. 4. Amateur sleuths—Fiction. I. Title

Ben Pecos Mystery Series.
Shelton, Connie, Ben Pecos mysteries.

BISAC : FICTION / Mystery & Detective.

813/.54

*To Susan Slater, who created such wonderful characters for the
Ben Pecos series and entrusted me to carry on her legacy.
I miss you, my dear friend.*

Chapter 1

The hurricane cast the conclusive vote. The fact that this storm was the third they'd endured in as many years only added to Ben and Julie's decision as they crouched beneath a mattress in the corner of their closet while it felt as if their house might crash down around them. It was one too many storms, after several sweltering summers. And then there was the time the alligator wandered into their yard while Julie was chasing a snake away from her lounger on the lanai.

The memory of the ferocious storm clung like a shadow. Wind howling like a banshee, tearing at the fabric of their lives. Rain slashing against windows, ripping at the roof and turning their home into a sieve filled with waterlogged furnishings. It was the last straw, one disaster too many, and as they surveyed the damage to their home and vehicles, so did the realization that they couldn't rebuild this time. Too many disappointments, too many battles with nature and bureaucracy alike.

The discussion about leaving Florida came in the aftermath, when the air was thick with mildew and uncertainty. And when the call came from Sanford Black, the clinical director of the Albuquerque Indian Health Service office, the man who'd hired and mentored Ben all those years ago, the solution to their dilemma fell into place. Ben's days as a roving psychologist, on call for a variety of tribes throughout the US, might be coming to an end. Hadn't Sandy stated that his coming back to New Mexico would be to take a permanent position? And if Ben wasn't mistaken, there was a hint that a decent promotion could come along. Ben and Julie agreed, life in the tropics was not for them.

New Mexico called to him, its wide-open vivid blue skies and red earth promising relief from the humid, cloying post-storm chaos. Ben had never been one to look back for too long, and yet the thought of the life they'd built—friends, routines, dreams now washed away— nagged slightly at him. He'd always been able to adapt, to move from one challenge to the next, but this transition felt different. It was both an ending and a beginning, one filled with new experiences and potential. The thought excited him after Sandy's call. A fresh start, a chance to reconnect with his roots, to work with the IHS in Albuquerque and make a tangible difference. The thought lit a fire within, pushing aside any sadness over leaving the Sunshine State.

He watched the receding landscape in the rearview mirror of the U-Haul as he cleared the traffic congestion in Orlando, and found himself wanting to press harder on the gas pedal, to cover the almost two-thousand miles as quickly as possible. This move back to New Mexico, returning to Tewa Pueblo, felt like both an escape and a return, leaving behind a world wrecked by storm chaos and political maneuvering. He took a deep breath, tasting freedom and the promise of a fresh start, and felt the road stretch endlessly ahead.

Reaching across to the passenger seat, he flipped open the lid of the small cooler Julie had packed, pulling out a bottle of guava juice and a packet of cheese crackers. The snack would keep him from having to stop until the truck needed gas. While he would have enjoyed taking a more scenic route, stopping at mom-and-pop diners in small towns, the sheer number of miles dictated that he stay on the interstate and make good time. Raven and the boys were meeting them in Albuquerque on Saturday. Julie was filing one final story for her editor at the *Herald* and would be flying in that evening. The logistics of getting everyone to the meet-up point at the Hotel Albuquerque was enough to make his head ache. Thank goodness for his petite, redheaded wife and her organizational skills.

As if he'd conjured her with his thoughts, his phone trilled and he saw her name on the screen. Activating the call hands-free, he asked what she was up to.

"They threw a party for me at the office," she said with a laugh. He could picture her red-gold curls, the hazel eyes and dark lashes. And those freckles, which had faded only slightly over the years. "There was a cake and everyone took turns praising my work. You know, the usual excuse for a bunch of busy reporters to take a break during the workday."

"Hey, your work deserves praise. I'm happy to hear

they appreciated you." Ben slowed the truck, noting signs for an upcoming construction zone. "So, what's next?"

"I'm still at it, I'm afraid. Dave wanted me to finish my current story. Says it's too late to assign it to someone else. Well, he couched that in praise for all the details he knows I have in my head, but basically didn't want to pay someone else overtime to get up to speed. It's fine. I don't mind. I may be rewriting on the plane and filing it from Albuquerque. Hopefully the hotel has decent wi-fi … I'm sure they do."

She kept talking as Ben navigated the narrow lane defined by orange barrels. "I need to do one more walk-through of the house on Dolphin Way, but I swear I'm turning the whole thing over to the insurance adjuster and the Realtor to work out what happens next. The insurance man's name is Dan Mahoney—seems sharp and somehow familiar. I think we've met him and his wife at some point."

A female voice was talking nearby and Ben could tell Julie was distracted. "I'll let you go," he said.

She murmured something in the way of agreement and the call ended. So many endings right now. He thought of his last days at the IHS office in Miami, watching as budget cuts gutted the programs he had put so much effort into. It was more than reorganization; it felt personal, although he knew it wasn't. In the end, the hurricane felt like an apt metaphor—sweeping away the past and leaving him no choice but to move on. This move to New Mexico was more than a physical relocation; it was a chance to rebuild both professionally and personally, to find his place in the world again.

Julie, ever supportive, knew how to ease his mind, make it all feel right, never voicing her own indefinite professional outcome. She still had journalistic contacts from their early days together in New Mexico, but there wasn't a job on the horizon yet. He needed to remain cognizant of her plans and needs too. This wasn't all about him.

* * *

Eight hours on the road and Ben was beat. He wasn't even out of Florida yet. The rented moving truck was not designed for his six-foot-two frame, and it felt as if every joint and muscle were screaming when he climbed out of the cab at the motel outside Tallahassee. Efficient Julie had reserved his room, requesting one on the ground floor with parking right outside. Still, Ben knew he wouldn't sleep well, knowing all their earthly possessions were in the back of that truck. And there were two more nights in hotels ahead of him.

He checked in and carried a bag of fast-food chicken and his shaving kit into the room. A hot shower, barely tasted food, and his head hit the pillow hard. His dreams became a mishmash of nonsensical images, remembered conversations, and uneasy anticipation.

He is standing among the adobe walls of the pueblo, the vibrant culture of his childhood, recalling some long-forgotten whispered secret. The scent of piñon smoke and sage waft toward him, and he sees that the adobe walls are painted gold by the setting sun, hears the soft padding of footsteps on dirt paths. Here, he realizes, is the place where the wisdom of his ancestors meets the pragmatism of his psychology textbooks. Yet, he had always embraced both, seeking ways to merge them into something meaningful, to help himself and others navigate the two worlds of Indian and Anglo. He realizes he is holding a letter in his hand—the job offer.

The air conditioner in the room kicked on and Ben rolled over, thinking he should check on the U-Haul. Walking to the window, he spread the curtain apart by one eye-width and looked out. The truck was there, seemingly undisturbed. Should he put his pants on, walk out to it, and check the doors? He didn't want to lose the fuzziness of sleep that still remained with him, so no. He made his way back to the bed and crawled back under the sheet. Minutes into his sleep, the dreams returned.

He's interviewing at the Indian Health Service office in Albuquerque but the interviewer isn't Sandy Black. He has to prove himself to the unfamiliar woman who is asking the questions. It's a chance to make a real impact on Pueblo Indian communities, to bring the skills he's honed back to the people who need them most, he tells her. This role isn't only about career advancement; it's about connecting, about making a difference that feels genuine and aligned with his values, his commitment, implementing programs that respect both traditional practices and modern methodologies. The very thought energizes him and he begins speaking faster, pushing aside doubts. He's ready to immerse himself in the work, he says, to be part of something larger. But the interviewer is noncommittal.

He walks out of the room, shaken. Did he say too much? Too little? Have he and Julie left their jobs for nothing? He goes back and gets the interviewer's attention, trying to explain to her about how balancing his professional identity with his cultural roots has been an ongoing tightrope walk he's never quite mastered. He tries to explain how determined he is to carve out his own space, a place where he can be both psychologist and Pueblo Indian.

Unexplainably, he's back at the pueblo but as a viewer this time. Summers he spent there, awkward among his cousins, wearing too-stiff clothes, learning the rhythms of community life. Those days stand stark against his school years in Utah, where everything felt alien and strange. The decision his grandmother made to send him away for a better education often filled him with resentment, yet he understands now what she sacrificed for his future. As he watches, grownup versions of his cousins tread the earthen streets between the conjoined adobe buildings. Ben wants to ask where they're going, what their plans are for the day.

Then he woke up. The bedside clock showed 4:51 a.m. He rolled over with a groan. He'd never get back to sleep now.

* * *

By the third day on the road, Ben felt the shift inside him as the miles flew by, a gradual letting go and the realization this move was actually happening. He'd left the deep South behind now, and the flat expanse of Texas prairies gave way to hints of mesas and the familiar contours of the Southwest.

The hum and motion of the U-Haul had settled into Ben's bones, making him wonder whether he would ever get his land-legs back. He'd talked to Julie a couple hours ago, reassured that she was at the Miami airport, on her way. Her warmth lingered, and he realized how much he'd missed her, how much he hated being alone in this damned truck for days on end. He missed the boys, too. Zac's ready smile and impish attitude, even at almost-seventeen. And Nathan, the Diné lad they'd adopted when his nearest relatives on the Navajo reservation died during the covid pandemic. Ben sincerely hoped that he'd get more frequent visitation now that he would not be a full continent away. Flights from Seattle to Albuquerque were reasonable and the boys old enough now to travel on their own. Getting this idea across to Raven might not be a slam-dunk, he realized.

Raven. For the life of him, Ben couldn't figure out what was behind her recent mood swings. Ever since their announcement that they were moving back west and wanted to see more of the boys, his ex-girlfriend—if a summer fling during college qualified as a real relationship—had gone from agreeable and cooperative to temperamental and moody.

When Ben posited to Julie that maybe Raven's drastic attitude switch was hormonal, Julie seemed skeptical. Still in her thirties, Raven was far too young to be entering menopause, surely. So, if not that, what was going on? A new man in her life? A downturn in her business? Something happening within the Takanni clan back in Moose Flats? But then again, hadn't she always been that way—her moods keeping everyone off balance?

Julie was the one who, quite kindly, suggested that maybe Raven was simply a mother who realized her son was growing up and would no longer be her little boy. And maybe she was right. Ben's psychology degree was supposed to have taught him all this stuff, but somehow it felt different when it was happening within his own circle.

He told himself he would have a nice, but professional, heart-to-heart with Raven when they saw each other this weekend.

The landscape shifted, and Ben's excitement built as he recognized the familiar contours of New Mexico. Driving now through mesas and high desert, the colors and textures sparked memories and emotions. The familiar shape of the Sandia Mountains loomed ahead; beyond that would be the Rio Grande Valley and the string of pueblos, reaching from a bit south of Albuquerque all the way north to Taos, those tiny communities that were still in place and inhabited for a thousand years or more. The feeling of homecoming was palpable, like a warm embrace after a long absence.

The sky was impossibly blue, the autumn air crisp and dry, and Ben breathed it in with a sense of belonging that ran deep. With the pull of his cultural roots, he was nearing the place where he felt most connected, most alive. And he was heading toward the life he was ready to start anew.

Heading home. And in that single thought, everything felt possible again.

Chapter 2

Julie Conlin Pecos sped through the terminal, a streak of fire against the Miami airport's glossy white tiles. She had missed enough flights to know when time was on her side and when it wasn't. Now was the latter, and she quickened her pace, lugging her laptop case, purse, and phone as she negotiated a clear path through the human obstacle course. Strands of red-gold hair slipped from the hasty knot on top of her head and clung to her damp neck. She'd ignored Miami's humidity for as long as she could, her thoughts set firmly on the next thing, the final story she would write for the *Herald*.

"We need more than speculation for the lead," she said to her office colleague on the phone, her tone professional.

The noise from the crowd forced her to press the earbud more firmly into her ear, and she nearly collided with a college kid in baggy shorts and a sleeveless t-shirt. She pivoted, neatly sidestepping him.

"Don't worry, I'll get it," she continued. "And make sure there are some decent archive photos that aren't too outdated."

Julie saw an information board and scanned it for her flight number. Gate change. She exhaled loudly and closed her eyes.

"You still there?" Her co-worker sounded young and hesitant, too deferential. Julie thought of her own early years on the national news circuit. She had been more aggressive, less apologetic.

"Yeah, I'm here. Just a minute." She looked again at the departures list, checking the new gate location and estimating her odds. She still had to clear the maze through security.

"Do you think this guy will talk to you?"

"Why don't you work on some feature filler, in case," Julie said. "Use yesterday's interviews with the Miccosukee folks, and hold tight. I'll get to it before it goes to layout anyway."

"We're all on edge, Julie. Editorial wants something soon."

"Tell them I'm en route. This evening, tops. And don't say anything about this story to anyone, especially not local news."

"We wouldn't do that."

"You know how this goes. Somebody blabs, it's all over by morning."

"Okay, okay."

Julie disconnected and rushed toward the TSA pre-check line, glad the *Herald* still paid for the expedited service. The gate change meant she would have to get through the lines with record speed. She fumbled for her boarding pass, crumpled and moist from her grip, and stood patiently as the agent compared the photo on her ID with the image of her face captured by the camera. A quick pass-through and she headed toward the shortest of the lines, reaching for the gray plastic bins she knew too well.

Julie stacked her phone beside her laptop and pulled the slender leather belt from the loops of her jeans. She passed through the detector, arms stretched, assuming the now-familiar posture of those who had spent too many recent years on planes. She'd no sooner picked up her armful of belongings from the conveyor than her phone rang again. This time it was the editorial assistant, number two in the newsroom, who launched immediately with questions.

"You'll have to keep stalling them," Julie said, pausing beside a bench on the other side of security to thread her belt back into its loops and reorganize everything. "Like I said, Becky's verifying a couple details for me. You'll have the story tonight or first thing in the morning, plenty of time for the afternoon edition."

"They're wondering if you're sure about this?"

"I'm sure," Julie said, confident about the story itself. She hoped every tiny detail was correct. If not, it was going to be a major embarrassment. On the upside, she would be all the way to New Mexico when the story broke.

She concentrated on the voice in her earbuds, listening as she organized her computer case, loading everything back into her pockets, and letting herself slip into hopefulness. By tomorrow morning, she would have filed the story, *and* she'd been promised the front page. Then she was done. She'd given her notice two weeks ago, practically begging for the chance to put this story to bed after more than a year of background research.

"All right," he said. "But don't say we didn't warn you if—"

Julie clicked off the connection before he could plant any more misgivings in her mind. Her eyes caught the overhead sign indicating the corridor she needed to take. She turned the corner, checked her watch, and knew she had five minutes of leeway. Ten at most.

Even with the *Herald*'s need to get this story on record and solid before anyone else picked it up, Julie was glad to get out of town exactly as planned. She slid the phone into her jeans pocket and broke into a slow jog.

Gate 37. Passengers were already filing into the jetway. She moved up to the counter, fidgeting with her boarding pass and distractedly wondering if she should try to get more details out of her reluctant Miami contacts.

Ten minutes later, Julie exhaled deeply and pressed her back against the thin blue cushion of the window seat, clutching her computer and notes like a mother hanging onto an unruly infant. She was one of the last passengers to board, and it showed in the overhead compartments—there had been no room left for anything more than her optimism.

"Everything okay, ma'am?" The flight attendant, an older woman with a kind face, gestured at the bulging laptop bag with a furrowed brow.

Julie nodded and slid her tote underneath the seat. "Fine, thanks."

"Let me know if I can do anything to help."

Julie nodded again, adjusting herself against the hard plastic trim of the window. The space around her was not exactly wide enough, but she'd gotten used to these kinds of temporary discomforts. She'd endured worse.

The plane pushed back from the gate, and she reined her thoughts to where she wanted them to stay—on the story, on getting a solid first draft written before she hit Albuquerque.

Three more hours, maybe a tad longer, with the way these airlines were running. She hoped the extra time would play in her favor, give her the leeway she needed to pull it all together. She powered up her laptop the moment after the announcement came that electronics could be used.

She set her earbuds and re-listened to the interviews she'd conducted over the past few months, her thoughts completely channeled. The material was impressive. Her story would be huge, a perfect sendoff as she left that job behind and began looking for another. Her editors would think they were crazy for doubting her.

Even before the beverage service began, Julie was well into her review of interview notes, key phrases she'd scrawled on index cards and tossed into her bag after the most recent meetings. Her mind scanned for details she knew were still lurking, the ones that would make a big splash when they surfaced.

She inserted questions on each card, anticipating what she'd need to clarify to pull the piece together. *Why now? What's his stake in this? Any other backing besides feds?*

On the laptop, she typed furiously for thirty minutes without stop. The bare bones of the story looked solid, but she needed more details, wanted to flesh it out. She closed her eyes and took three deep breaths, clearing her head for a minute by concentrating on the logistics of the trip.

Albuquerque arrival 4:10, rent car, get to hotel.

Ben would be arriving in Albuquerque soon. Or maybe

not quite yet. And what about Raven and the boys? As she understood the plan, the kids were on autumn break from their boarding school in Bellingham, joining Raven in Seattle, and the three were driving down to New Mexico. Julie thought she remembered there was to be one overnight stop on the way.

Truthfully, she didn't much care what Raven did. Zac's mother wasn't her biggest fan, and the sentiment was mutual. But she and Ben were both looking forward to spending the week with Zac and Nathan, and hoping to get more of the holidays together now that they were settling in the Southwest again. She remembered how Zac had asked, with naïve curiosity, whether "the married parents" were going to be together this time.

Julie blinked the thought away, re-focusing on her draft. Grabbing important details was an advantage when she was in investigative mode, a far different job than when she'd first begun working at the *Herald* as lifestyle editor. And these leads had panned out better than she hoped. *Nothing is coincidental,* she'd jotted on the back of another index card, and followed it with a list of events, time-stamped in short dashes.

5:00 a.m. K's info?

8:30. Meet C & L—confirm or bluff?

11:15. Suspect back in Miami. Paperwork?

1:45. Extra witness? Change story?

3:20. Possible sighting. Big Q.

No idea whether that tip would turn out solid or not. She'd know as soon as she got word from her fact-checker back in Miami. The pieces could fall apart in the next twelve hours, and she needed to hedge the risk by pushing everything to her editor sooner than later. From a back page in her notebook, a photo slipped out. Ben.

The picture was a selfie he'd printed for her—Ben with his deep brown eyes, dark hair not quite touching his collar, she barely coming up to his shoulder. His slender fingers draped over her shoulder. They'd taken it on their anniversary, in a restaurant where the dessert was photo-worthy. Both were smiling widely and her heart gave a thump, seeing his face. She loved this man completely, although she had to admit his judgment could become skewed when it came to family matters. Especially now that he had two sons he wanted to know, to be a part of their lives.

She hoped they had time for even half the activities they'd talked about during this trip. They couldn't forget that Nathan might also want to take time to reconnect with his own Diné people while he was in New Mexico.

The sky outside her window smoothed into a translucent pale blue, with a smear of cloud in the distance. Julie sat up straighter. "Okay, back to work," she muttered.

She'd already mentally composed the next paragraph of her draft, settling her brain as she typed the words. When the flight attendant returned with an offer of drinks or snacks, Julie shook her head, murmuring something that wasn't a real word and only half polite. She moved from her computer's keyboard back to the index cards, muttering under her breath. "This could be huge, huge, huge…"

The man in the seat next to her had watched her sort through notes and talk to herself for long enough to give in to the impulse to speak. "I don't want to bug you, but my brother's in news. KXAA, out in Phoenix. You with TV or print?"

"Print," she said. "And freelance, these days." It was

the answer she'd settled upon, one that sounded better than unemployed-at-the-moment.

"Oh. Well, then maybe you should talk to him. Station's always looking to hire."

"Thanks," she said, "but I'm—"

"Yeah, you've got a deadline." He turned to the woman on his other side, something about her willingness to share pretzels and beer more promising than Julie's distracted replies.

Julie went back to her work, content that phone reception was still well over an hour away, and her *Herald* co-worker would soon be pulling together the photos she needed.

Editorial wouldn't be this nervous if they didn't know she was on the verge of a major scoop. It was that kind of micro-managing that had driven her away from New York's cutthroat news scene, years ago, where both professional and personal lives competed for top billing. Two a.m. phone calls. Those she'd gotten used to, but she was more than happy to be out of that world. A more laid-back atmosphere held a lot of appeal.

She glanced again out the tiny window and saw the plane's wing suspended in a sky that had changed subtly. Much like the elements she felt surrounding her story. The story she had yet to complete, she reminded herself.

She knew she could have gone back to New Mexico without finalizing this last Miami connection, could have handed it off to another reporter. Jake Pacheco would have run with it in a heartbeat. Did they need her extra week of chasing spooks, of tracking down feds who might know more than they should about what had been going on? But in the end, she'd made this commitment and would stick with it.

The screen's white light reflected on her face as she drafted one, two, then three potential leads. Some of her notes from earlier started looking more cohesive.

Nudge into column format. Leave three paragraphs open for more details. Push before midnight.

Even if she didn't hit the soft deadline, her draft would come close enough that the editors wouldn't panic. They'd all agreed—this was too important a story to skimp on it. Better right than rushed. Even if it didn't get finalized before landing, she'd be back on track once they refueled in Dallas.

Two more hours, tops.

Chapter 3

Ben leaned back in his chair, taking in the untouched basket of tortilla chips and his own half-finished beer, as Sandy's latest tale wound to a close. They'd covered the basics: How did it feel to be back? To be this close to the community Ben had once called home?

Ben spoke slowly, still processing the complex emotions as he got used to being back in Albuquerque, only an hour-plus from the pueblo, looking forward to reconnecting with his Tewa roots, thinking about the best ways to blend pueblo tradition with modern demands, to help each of the tribes. Truthfully, he wanted to handle the discussion with Sandy far more adeptly than he'd bumbled through the interview in his crazy dream.

"It's been years since I've spent much time here. Being so close to the pueblo will be like revisiting a piece of myself I haven't seen in a long time." He picked up his glass, more to keep his hands busy than anything else. "I want to do this right," he said finally. "For Julie, for me, for the boys. My cultural heritage is a part of that. But it's not simple. It never has been."

Sandy nodded with a smile. "I remember that. Your unique upbringing."

"Unique. That's a great word for it." Ben felt grateful for Sandy's understanding.

"As we discussed on the phone, the job involves your heading up the mental health unit for the entire 19 Pueblos District. I'm sure you've thought carefully about that, and are you ready for it?" Sandy asked gently.

"Absolutely." Ben smiled and nodded, appreciating the way Sandy always seemed to grasp the bigger picture. He glanced out the window of the cozy neighborhood bar, where the setting sun had turned the face of the Sandias their unusual 'watermelon' color.

"Being back might not be as straightforward as you're hoping." Sandy's tone added a dash of reality. He took a sip of his beer before continuing. "When I first started working with the pueblo communities, I thought my time with the CDC and Indian Health Services had prepared me. But blending into a community is different from studying it. As an Anglo, I had to learn that the hard way."

Ben nodded, appreciating the older man's honesty. Ben's own half-Indian, half-Anglo heritage had often been a disadvantage when he was a kid, but now it might be a benefit.

"It's easy to see things from a distance and think you know what you're getting into," Sandy said. "But when you're living it every day, there's a lot you don't expect. You do realize you'd make a lot more money as a psychologist if you opened a private practice?"

Ben waved off the question. "At least my student loans are repaid now, and I'd rather devote my career to something that helps my people."

"You're a doctor—you know all this—but the key is patience," Sandy added. "And understanding. Don't expect everything to fall into place immediately."

"It's nice to hear you say that," Ben said. "I've been trying to remind myself to take it slowly. But sometimes, knowing the extent of what needs to be done makes it hard to wait."

Sandy's expression softened.

"I think you're already miles ahead by recognizing that," he said. "It's a delicate balance, but you've got the right instincts. And you've gained a lot of experience during the years since you were an intern in my office."

Ben paused, letting the reassurance settle. "Thanks, Sandy," he said. "Really. It helps more than you know."

Sandy gave him a warm smile, deflecting the gratitude in his typical fashion. Then his expression grew more serious. "You know, Ben, I'm not getting any younger. There's talk in the agency about you eventually taking over the office, inheriting my job. Even nationwide, IHS is doing a much better job of bringing tribal members into top positions. It's about time they phased out old white men like me. Seriously."

Ben straightened. "You're not retiring anytime soon, are you? I mean, there's nothing ... health-wise?"

"Not at all. But, Ben, you've got the vision and the drive, and maybe I'll start limiting my *drives* to those on the golf course one of these days. I'm not saying it'll be anytime soon, but we might start laying the groundwork together. See how we can make the transition smooth. When the time comes."

Ben's pulse raced, the idea of leading the office suddenly so real he could almost touch it. His thoughts flitted through dozens of ideas. "I'd like to see us start incorporating more traditional methods alongside the modern ones."

Sandy's eyes sparkled at the suggestion. "That's exactly why I want you to do this. You understand both sides. Bridging those approaches could change lives."

Suddenly, the scope of what lay ahead felt both thrilling and overwhelming. He tried to envision the impact he could have, what it would mean to the community. And to himself.

"Please know you've got my support every step of the way," Sandy said.

"I've learned so much from you," Ben said. "Having you believe in me … it means a lot."

"You're more than ready for this next step," Sandy said. "You're capable and you care. That's what counts."

Ben allowed himself to believe it. He had worked hard for this.

"This work changes lives," Sandy said. "And not only the lives of our patients."

"I have to admit I have selfish motives as well. I hear from my aunt that a cousin isn't doing well. Vicente was always the wild child among us—drinking, speeding, acting out his pent-up anger. Frankly, he was a bit of a bully to me, the younger one. I hope now I can get to know the adult version, see what's going on with him, figure out some helpful options for him."

Sandy nodded. "I'm sure you'll be a huge help, to your family and so many others."

Ben let the words resonate, thinking about the long journey that had led him here. From the challenges of his childhood, balancing his mixed heritage, the unsettled life of being sent to work with various tribes throughout the nation, to this moment of convergence where everything seemed to align.

"I was worried about making this move," Ben admitted. "But it feels like the right place. The right time."

"Your history and your training—it's a rare combination," Sandy said. "You've got insights no one else does. Keep trusting that."

Sandy raised his glass. "To new beginnings, and the exciting journey ahead."

Ben clinked his glass against Sandy's, the sound clear and full of promise. Despite his earlier fatigue from the four days on the road, he felt renewed, buoyed by the conversation. It was a path of challenges, yes, but also of unimaginable potential.

Sandy dropped some cash on the table, saying both the beer and the conversation were his treat. Together, they walked out into the gathering dusk. Sandy's pickup truck sat in the parking lot; Ben's hotel was across the street, half a block north. Outside, he savored the chill of October, took a deep breath of the high desert air, invigorating and bracing.

"So, I'll see you a week from Monday at the office?" Sandy pulled his keys from the pocket of his jeans.

"Absolutely. I promised Julie and the boys a drive up to Tewa. Aunt Zena swears she is itching to cook for us. By the time we unpack our household things, I will be more than ready to start my new work." Ben paused at the edge of the parking lot. "Sandy, I can't thank you enough."

Sandy gave a quick nod, then climbed into his truck and started it.

Ben waited on the sidewalk at the corner for the pedestrian symbol to light up then crossed Rio Grande Boulevard and strode toward the Hotel Albuquerque. New responsibilities. New opportunities. New beginnings! He stepped into the beautifully ornate hotel lobby, excitement simmering at the thought of Julie arriving.

Inside the quiet elevator, Ben felt the anticipation quicken in his chest. Julie would be here any minute. He imagined her expression, the way her eyes would light up when he told her the news. He could hardly wait to share every detail of the conversation. About Sandy's plans for retirement. About the future they would build together back here at home.

As the elevator dinged closer to his floor, Ben thought of how Julie had stood by him, a constant support. He felt a surge of gratitude so strong it took his breath. She had quit a prestigious and lucrative job with a major newspaper, a sacrifice he couldn't ever forget. Her belief in him never wavered, even when he questioned himself.

Ben pictured her, that familiar warmth in her voice, the easy way she made everything seem possible. His heart was full with the anticipation of seeing her, and of seeing his boys, of sharing this new beginning. The doors opened, and he stepped out, heading toward their room with a buoyancy that felt like flight.

All he needed now was for her to walk through the door.

Chapter 4

Albuquerque's sunsets had always amazed her. Julie's dad used to say it was because of the way the light caught dust particles in the air, but she didn't recall many dirt roads anymore. The city was as paved and built-up as most others, but she liked the story and loved the vivid oranges and yellows in the sky. She made her way through the newly renovated terminal, filled with amazing examples of local art and Albuquerque's long history with aviation, toward the baggage claim. While she stood at the carousel, she texted Ben to say she'd arrived and would be at the hotel as soon as she retrieved her bag and her rental car.

The plan was to use the compact vehicle for running around town and for the day trip up to Tewa tomorrow, rather than clunking around in the U-Haul. Once they unloaded boxes at their apartment, the truck would get returned. And soon, they would need to get busy shopping for a vehicle or two of their own. The insurance company had paid enough for her nearly new, now obliterated, BMW that she should be able to get something decent to replace it.

Travelers from another flight formed a cluster near the carousels, slipping into jackets against the cooler air, wondering whether their layers would be enough against the approaching October chill. Julie, glad to have swapped cotton for fleece as she left the plane, skirted around them, grabbed her bag, and made her way outside.

The change in air, in scent, in feel, reminded her that the desert was not far in the distance. She had left Miami too recently to know for sure how New Mexico's actual winter would feel. But that was still weeks away.

She boarded a van to the car rental lot and checked her text messages during the two-minute ride. One from Ben: I've got some great news. Raven and the boys should be here any minute.

She hoped he didn't think that was the great news, but she sent him a thumbs-up emoji anyway. The other six messages were business, calls from the *Herald*. From the desk. Maybe from the lawyers, wondering about liability if she went public before her story could be thoroughly vetted. She could field all those calls soon, but would rather have some dinner and reread the article before she responded with specifics.

Julie picked up her paperwork and moved into the dimly lit rental car section of the parking lot, only half distracted by thoughts of what she might be missing from the east coast, and what she might be missing from Ben. She found her assigned car. Why did it always seem she got one with out-of-state plates, never blending in with the locals? Oh well, it would serve its purpose. She stashed her things in the trunk and started the car, setting up the map on her phone to give directions to the hotel.

The phone pinged with a message, startling her. The others are here. Hungry. Meet us at La Hacienda.

She knew where that was, in Old Town, only a couple blocks from the hotel. It would be easier to snag a parking spot at the hotel while other guests were out for the evening, and the short walk would do her good after hours of confinement on the plane. She sent Ben a quick response then forced herself to concentrate on the twenty-minute drive in rush hour traffic.

Julie wasn't sure how she felt about having Ben's ex and kids here the very minute they returned to the city, but had decided she wanted to let him handle it all on his own. Let him be the sole organizer of how they would fit together, how his past with Raven and his newer role as a father would work itself out. But she also wanted to be there, to be sure that Ben wouldn't assume it was his sole responsibility. They were in this together.

All in all, she was glad to be back. Torn but glad, with a clear plan to fulfill her final commitment to the *Herald* and also this new one to Ben, as they settled into yet another lifestyle. In the aftermath of the hurricane—before her current assignment had consumed her life, before this pop-up plan involving two teens on autumn break from school—she'd explored homes for sale in Albuquerque, and she had some news for Ben on that subject. But first, she rehearsed the way she'd tell him that the newspaper assignment wasn't actually finished; she would address that once they were alone.

Chapter 5

Ben's phone vibrated with a message. He had half expected Raven to cancel at the last minute. She hadn't—a relief. Then excitement, nerves, tension—the whole buzzing mix of emotion that always came along with seeing his boys. He jogged toward the elevator, imagining the scene below, the moments he would share with Zac and Nathan. Family. He spotted them even before he reached the lobby, waiting at the check-in desk. Raven's unmistakable presence, Zac and Nathan flanking her like sentinels. Ben felt warmth bloom through his veins when Zac spotted him. Nathan waved. Raven turned, her face unreadable.

He walked faster at the sight of the boys. "Hey! Over here!" Zac called, pulling Nathan's arm.

"Good to see you both," Ben said as he approached,

trying to meet both their eyes at once. Zac rushed forward, all arms and energy, while Nathan offered a more restrained but genuine smile. "You've still got your shell bracelet, I see."

Nathan pointed at the strand of sinew with tiny white shells on Zac's wrist. It came from Alaska but Zac had given it to Nathan a few years ago, to symbolize the fact that they were best friends and then brothers. "We share it back and forth now."

Ben hugged Zac, noticing the kid's growth, both in stature and confidence. "You've shot up even more since the last time I saw you."

"I'm almost taller than you!" Zac beamed, stepping back.

"You wait," Nathan said with a teasing grin. "Next year, I'll be the tallest."

Ben laughed, ruffling Nathan's hair as he released Zac. "I'll need to start eating my spinach to catch up." He looked at Raven, who remained at the desk, now tapping the screen of her phone. Her distance didn't surprise him. Ben kept his focus on the boys, though his glance lingered, assessing her mood.

"Was the trip okay?" he asked, careful to include Raven in the conversation while giving her room to join at her own pace.

Zac jumped in eagerly, his voice a quick stream of words. "It was awesome. We saw the gigantic-est donut shop ever in Portland, and then this cool diner in Salt Lake City with, like, a million kinds of pie."

"The trip wasn't exactly fast," Nathan added, more even-keeled. "But it wasn't rainy. A nice break from Bellingham."

Ben caught Raven's eye. Her smile was brief, a flash

before it faded back to the usual guarded expression.

"It was a marathon," she said, sarcasm coating her words. "And I'm the one who lost."

Zac laughed, unaware of the sting. Ben noted the undercurrent but he let it slide, focusing instead on Zac and Nathan's enthusiasm.

"We didn't even have to stop in Utah for anything longer than pie," Zac continued. "And Mom let us do all the driving."

Nathan smirked. "Not quite. But it was long enough that she almost fell asleep a few times."

"I told you those donuts were monsters," Raven said. "Sugar coma."

Her dry humor brought a reluctant smile to Ben's face. He caught her eye again, this time offering a look of gratitude.

"I'm glad you're all here," Ben said. "Really."

Nathan nodded, his eyes softening as he looked at Ben. "It's cool to be back."

Zac bounced again, a quick, joyful motion that spoke more than words. Ben wanted to absorb every detail, memorize these first moments and hold onto them.

He gestured toward the elevators. "How about we let you guys get settled? Julie and I are right on the same floor." He took the handle of Raven's suitcase and let himself hope that the visit would unfold smoothly, that the time together would reinforce the connections that mattered most.

"I hope it wasn't too much," he said, his tone careful but sincere. "I know the drive was a stressor. It means a lot."

Raven looked at him sideways, assessing. "Well," she

said with a hint of a smile, "it wasn't quite the Iditarod."

Ben chuckled, the tension easing ever so slightly. "Glad you didn't have to use the dogsled."

They walked a tad closer, still a cautious distance but with the unspoken agreement to keep it civil. Ben watched Zac and Nathan ahead of them, glad to see that the boys were still best friends.

"We're all super happy to be here," Zac said, spinning around to face them while still walking. "And the trip was actually kind of fun."

Raven raised an eyebrow. "You might change your mind about road trips after we head back."

Ben smiled, sensing the shift in mood, however slight.

As they approached the elevator, Ben glanced at Raven, gauging her expression one last time. The boys were already on board, pressing buttons and jostling each other, their deepening voices echoing in the metal space. Ben wanted to believe that this was the beginning of something positive.

He turned to the boys, a warm look in his eyes. "So," he said, "ready for the adventure?"

Zac nodded, wide-eyed and eager. Nathan leaned against the wall, more understated but every bit as committed.

"We're up for it," Nathan said, giving Zac a playful nudge.

Ben held the door open for Raven, letting her pass inside before following.

"That's the spirit," he said, closing the door.

They reached their floor. Ben sensed some kind of quiet discontent simmering under Raven's words and tight smile. Co-parenting, he thought, with miles in between them—not the easiest for anyone. The distance and its difficulties hummed through their exchanges like an old transmission line. He let it be for now. The boys bounded into the room, their voices a wild jumble of excitement, their bags tossed across the beds. Energy bounced off the walls. Ben watched, hope rising as he steered Raven's suitcase to a spot near the tall entertainment center.

Nathan's eyes shone with anticipation. "Do we get to see the pueblo tomorrow?" he asked.

Ben loved the spark of curiosity. He'd promised Nathan a stop at Tewa during a road trip the two had done together, but events in South Dakota along the way had derailed it. And his idea of spending time at Tewa with Zac got postponed during the pandemic when they'd ended up working on the Navajo rez instead. He couldn't regret that part; it was when they'd first met the recently orphaned Nathan. But he had long wished he had more time with the boys, and he intended to remedy that soon.

"That's the plan," Ben said. "I'll take you around, show you the sights. We've got plenty of time."

Zac beamed, and Nathan threw a pillow across the room, just missing Zac's head.

"Stop it!" Zac laughed, diving onto the bed with Nathan in pursuit. The sound of their scuffle filled the space with familiar noise, a reminder of summers and shared adventures.

"Guys, guys … watch the running. There are probably other guests in the room below this one." Raven watched them, leaning against the dresser, arms crossed. Her expression shifted between fondness and the tension Ben knew all too well.

"They're excited," he said, his tone betraying his

tiredness from the long drive. He chose to focus on the positives. "It's going to be a good visit. I've got a lot planned for them."

Zac popped up, hair a mess, eyes shining. "We're seeing Lorenzo, right?"

The mention of Lorenzo sent a pang through Ben, an echo of loss and the tradition he hoped to pass on. "Yes," Ben said. "We'll pay our respects at the cemetery. Maybe even see some of the places Lorenzo loved."

Nathan added his own quiet voice. "Will we get to watch any dances?"

Ben felt his hopes swell, knowing their interest was genuine. "There might be some at the end of the week," he said. "Let's play it by ear."

"I bet none of the guys my age at Tewa ever participated in a Lakota sun dance."

"You're probably right, Nathan, but let's see how it plays out before you mention that, right?"

They quieted for a moment; Zac seemed thoughtful, absorbing everything. Ben watched, hoping the boy's intense focus was as meaningful as it seemed.

"There's so much I want to show you," Ben said. "I want you both to feel connected."

Nathan and Zac exchanged a look, then Zac spoke up. "We'll learn it all, Dad. Promise."

Ben glanced at Raven, catching a glimpse of something in her expression before she masked it.

"There's a lot more we can do around here, too," Ben added. "Sandia Peak has a tram to the top, and the Balloon Fiesta is starting. Maybe even a trip to Santa Fe if there's time."

Zac nodded enthusiastically. Nathan leaned back, more

relaxed than before.

Ben realized how fast their week together could slip away. But he also felt the sense that this was a moment they'd all remember.

The boys began unpacking in a blur of clothes and noise. Zac pulled out a stuffed coyote and set it on his pillow, earning a playful shove from Nathan. "He still sleeps with that thing," Nathan teased.

"It's my lucky charm," Zac shot back with a grin. "By the way, I'm hungry!"

Raven watched, her gaze softening despite her earlier reservations.

"How about I leave you to freshen up?" Ben suggested. "Shall we meet downstairs in fifteen minutes?"

"Dinner in Old Town?" Nathan guessed.

Ben nodded, pleased at Nathan's recollection. "Exactly. I thought we'd start with some New Mexican food at La Hacienda."

Zac tossed a shirt onto Nathan's bed. "I want green chile everything!"

Raven gave a reluctant smile. "Oh boy. They'll be eating breakfast burritos for life."

Ben felt a grin spreading across his face. "At least they'll never go hungry."

Raven held his gaze, the tension losing its sharp edge.

"Let's talk after we eat," Ben said, careful to keep his tone neutral as he turned toward the door. "I think we should focus on the visit, especially for Zac and Nathan."

Raven gave a nod, her agreement not so much a concession as a shared desire for peace. Ben let it be enough for now.

He turned to the boys, capturing their attention once

more. "You guys get ready and I'll see you downstairs," Ben said. He opened the door, catching one last look at them. Nathan tossed another pillow at Zac, and laughter filled the room, pushing out the last of Ben's worries.

As he stepped into the hallway, he heard Zac call out with a hint of mischief. "Wait till you hear about the train!" The door closed behind him before he could ask what that was about.

Fifteen minutes later, he settled onto one of the chairs in the lobby and fired off a quick text to Julie about the dinner plan. He'd hoped she would have time to come here first, but as he watched the sky unfurl its colors—the fiery oranges dissolving into purple-blue—he suggested meeting at the restaurant instead. That way, he wouldn't have to keep two hungry teens waiting.

Exactly on time, Zac and Nathan darted forward from the bank of elevators, full of life and laughter, leaving Raven in their wake. They crossed the lobby to the front door, and Ben let them stride ahead while he held the door for Raven. Her eyes met his, searching for any hint of disagreement, but he offered none. They both knew he wanted to discuss a more equal custody arrangement, but now was not the right moment for that. They needed this moment of unspoken truce.

They headed toward Old Town, the adobe buildings soft against the desert evening. Ben felt the air cool around them, crisp in comparison with Florida. The scents of piñon smoke and chile, made him think of childhood. He wanted Zac and Nathan to feel that same connection, hoped it would settle into their bones and stay there.

The boys walked ahead, voices carrying through the night. Their excitement was contagious, pulling Ben into their orbit. He matched his pace to Raven's, testing the waters.

"You always have this much energy?" he called to Zac, watching the teen's restless pace.

"Yep, always!" Zac shouted back, laughing. Nathan gave him a friendly shove.

"We need to get you on the basketball court, run off some of that excess," Ben teased.

He stole a look at Raven, her face unreadable again. He wondered what she was thinking, whether this visit could change things or if it would only open old wounds. They kept moving, crossing the street and heading toward the restaurant.

The red strands of chile lights blinked in welcome, and Ben remembered meals there when he was in college. He hoped Zac and Nathan would make their own memories here, as well.

"Does Julie know we're coming?" Raven asked, her tone casual but with an edge. For the most part, they all got along. But sharing Zac with anyone else, even his own father, had always been a sore spot.

"She knows and she's on the way," Ben said, his voice steady. "She's looking forward to seeing you. All of you."

They reached the door, Zac and Nathan pushing through, their voices a happy echo. Ben held the entrance open, still trying to gauge when and how to broach the custody question. For now, it could wait.

The place buzzed with life, tourists and locals sharing the warm space. Ben loved the feel of it, the way it reminded him of community. Of connection. Zac and Nathan followed the hostess to a table near the back. The adults caught up with them, Ben letting Raven choose her seat, then taking a chair across from Nathan and leaving one beside him open for Julie.

"Order anything you want," Ben said, pushing the menus toward the boys. "Just remember we can't eat twenty pounds of sopapillas."

Zac grinned, already plotting his strategy. "What if we finish our dinner and want that many, anyway?"

Nathan joined in, his voice full of mock seriousness. "I think I could eat forty pounds."

Ben laughed, the sound full and genuine. "Julie and I might need to bring reinforcements to handle that many," Ben said. When he caught a glimpse of his reflection in the restaurant's mirrored wall, he saw himself surrounded by family, the picture both comforting and somewhat precarious.

He caught sight of Julie's figure moving toward them, her hair a flame against the subdued light. He waved her over, and the boys' faces lit up as she approached.

"Did I hear something about forty pounds of sopapillas?" Julie asked, sliding into the chair next to Ben. "How was the trip?" she asked, directing the question to everyone at the table.

Ben let the conversation swirl around him, his thoughts focused both on Zac and Nathan—their stories and laughter loud and real—but also on Raven. She was the wildcard, the one who could tip the balance of this visit from connection to conflict.

The waiter arrived, bringing water, baskets of chips, and bowls of salsa. Ben watched as Zac and Nathan ordered. He let them lead the way, enjoying their ease.

With the boys distracted, Raven faced Ben. "You've got a lot planned. You want to make them stay, don't you?"

Tread lightly, he reminded himself. "I want the boys to have a say in where they are, now that they're older."

She held his eyes for a moment longer, then turned to Julie with a slight shift in tone. "And you're okay with that? The kids spending so much time in your hair?"

Julie responded without missing a beat. "They love spending time with Ben. And I think they'll love being in New Mexico."

Raven's eyes flicked between them, assessing the united front. "It's a long way from home for them," she said, her tone losing some of its sharpness.

Ben could sense the tide turning, but knew better than to count on anything. "Let's see how this trip goes."

Julie placed a gentle hand on his arm, a silent vote of confidence. Raven leaned back in her chair, taking a quick glance at her phone before jamming it into her pocket.

The food arrived, heaping plates of enchiladas and chile rellenos. Zac and Nathan dug in, teasing each other over who could handle the hottest sauce. The noise and chaos were comforting to Ben, like a protective shield against the harder conversations that loomed beyond this night.

They laughed and teased, a picture of family. But Ben felt the ticking clock, the knowledge of how temporary it might be. He wanted to hold onto this, to stretch it out and let it last forever.

As the plates cleared and the meal wound down, he turned toward the other end of the table. "We should make it an early night since we've got a big day tomorrow, guys. It's gonna be great," he said, as much to himself as to the rest of them.

Zac yawned theatrically. "Think we'll have any energy

left for dancing?" he asked, a mischievous look in his eye.

"Not after you eat all those sopapillas," Ben said, pointing to the basket that still held a few of the puffed pastries.

They gathered their things, Zac and Nathan stumbling over each other as they pushed out of their chairs.

As they all stepped into the night, Ben allowed himself to believe, at least for now, that this visit would change everything.

Chapter 6

Back in their room, silence wrapped around Ben and Julie like a soft cocoon, an antidote to the vibration of the road and the noise of the rowdy boys. Ben felt the pressure valve release as he closed the door. Julie unzipped her bag and carried her toiletry kit to the bathroom. "Think this visit will be as smooth as you're hoping?" she asked, peering through the doorway.

"I don't know," he admitted, rubbing his neck, the tension of the past few days slipping away beneath his touch. "I thought we were getting somewhere, then she brought up Zac's time away from Alaska, as we got off the elevator."

Julie squirted toothpaste onto her toothbrush. "Raven's got her own ideas of what's best," she said, a slight edge to her voice. "You've got yours."

Ben nodded, turning to his own overnight bag. It wasn't only about differing opinions. It was about cultures, expectations, and the constant tug-of-war he felt between them. Was Raven becoming more difficult with the passing years, or had he begun to expect better cooperation? "Sometimes it feels like the kids are caught in the middle." But weren't they always, in these situations?

Julie turned toward the bathroom mirror, watching his movements. "They know you're there for them, Ben. You and Raven might not always agree, but you both love them."

Ben sat on the bed, giving her time to finish her bathroom routine. He thought about the years spent piecing together a family across so many miles. It was hard, trying to keep the kids connected to the New Mexico part of their heritage without making Raven feel like she was losing them. And he must admit that he'd not done the best job of that, taking assignments all over the country, jobs that didn't always coincide with school holidays.

Julie stepped out of the bathroom, her freckles glowing, her eyes and skin free of makeup now. As if she'd heard his thoughts she said, "That connection is why this trip is so important."

"It's the first step," he said. "A way to show Zac where we come from, and where both boys fit in."

Julie smiled, a gentle reassurance. "It's more than a first step, Ben. It's a path you've been on since the day Zac came into your life."

Ben let the truth of that sink in as he brushed his teeth. This wasn't merely about a week in New Mexico. It was about laying the foundation for something more, something that could last.

"They'll see how much it matters," he said, conviction

in his voice as he turned out the bathroom light and undressed.

Julie nodded, pulling back the covers on the king-sized bed and settling in beside him. "And so will Raven."

Ben hoped she was right, knowing how much hung in the balance. He thought about the next day, the visit to the pueblo, the way he'd imagined it playing out in his mind so many times. "I want it to feel right," he said, his voice softening. "For everyone."

Julie curled into him. "I think it will."

Ben laid back and took a deep breath. He imagined Zac and Nathan at Tewa, seeing it through their eyes, letting the pueblo culture and their extended family connect with them in ways he couldn't quite predict but desperately hoped for.

They settled under the covers, the night stretching out before them, the weariness of the day settling heavy in their bones.

"We'll make it work," Ben's voice carried softly, optimistic.

Julie squeezed his hand. He stared toward the ceiling, the darkness a welcome comfort, and thought about the dramatic changes in their lives in the month since the storm, the long road they'd all traveled to reach this point, and the uncharted territory that stretched beyond it.

"Get some sleep," Julie said, her voice a soothing lull. "Tomorrow's gonna be huge."

Ben smiled into the dark at her gentle command. He let his eyes close. It *was* going to be huge. Ben felt that deep down. When Julie's soft breathing turned to the regular rhythm of sleep, he rolled over, willing the buzz of the highway out of his system.

And then his phone vibrated.

His first thought was about the new job. Maybe Sandy Black had more information for him. At nine-thirty p.m.? But no. It was Raven.

He slipped quietly out of bed and carried the phone into the bathroom to check the text. We need to agree on the holiday plans. Better to talk about that without the boys around.

Seriously, now? But she was right that it was probably better for the adults to be in agreement before broaching the subject with the kids. He began thumbing the keyboard. Can we meet in the lobby? I don't have the energy for a lot of texting.

So much for sleep, Ben thought as he stepped back into the khaki pants he'd worn all day and pulled his black tee shirt over his head. He had planned to let the night fade away, let his mind drift into rest. Don't let her get you wound up, he told himself as he picked up a room key and let himself out into the hall. With luck he would get this over with and be back in bed without disturbing poor Julie. She'd been working her tail off for weeks now and needed her rest.

Raven was waiting in the lobby, near the front doors. She looked even fresher than she had an hour ago, her black tresses brushed and gleaming. Her elbow-length shirt revealed only a few of her tattoos, Haida designs with special meaning to her tribe. "Nathan left his bag in the car," she said. "Walk out with me and I'll grab it while we talk."

"Sure, whatever." Ben finger-combed his hair, wondering how disheveled he looked. At least a walk to the parking lot would give him a chance to make sure the U-Haul was securely locked.

He followed her, noticing her sedan was parked next

to the rented truck. Convenient, anyway. After tugging on each of the truck's door handles, he walked over and stood at the back of her car, where she was digging through a crowded jumble of sleeping bags, zipper cases, a spare tire, a tool bag, and two small Igloo coolers.

"Nathan's bag is a dark blue one," she muttered, still pawing through the clutter.

"So, about the holidays?" His patience was wearing thin.

"Our agreement was always that you got them a month during the summer, and they stayed with me throughout the school year."

"Yes, and now that Julie and I are so much closer, we'd love to have them with us for part of the winter break." What he'd proposed, more than a week ago, was that they alternate Thanksgiving and Christmas, then split the summer months. "There was a big difference from when Zac was ten and the plane flight was six hours. Two teens on a three-hour flight is much more doable."

She plucked a bag from the truck and turned toward him. "No go. We have Iditarod practice throughout December and January. I'm taking them up to my brother's place in Moose Flats so we can get the dogs ready. Zac has been completely into this for years now."

"And he wants to do it again this year?"

"I'm sure he does. Romo's probably competing for the last time this year."

Ben smiled, recalling the malamute pup Zac loved so much. "But have you asked him? Have you even told him about my other idea?"

From her expression he could tell she hadn't.

He leaned against the bumper of the truck, took a

deep breath, and tried another approach. "Okay. Let's not rush into a decision. How about if the boys come here at Thanksgiving, and then we'll talk about plans for the longer break in December?"

"We have to plan ahead. This isn't fair to the boys."

"Fair would be for us to ask them. They're definitely old enough to have a say, even though we still have parental authority." His control slipped. "And don't forget, Nathan is legally mine, adopted here in New Mexico."

Her fist clenched the handle of the duffle bag and her face became a mask of fury. "You'd split them up? Nathan is Zac's best friend, and that's the whole reason he's been living with me. They'd hate you forever."

Low blow. He turned away, paced a dozen steps, and walked back.

She was on a roll. "If you cared about the boys, you'd go along with what we've always done."

"Raven, you're the one making this difficult. Why do you always have to make things so hard?" Even as the words slipped out, he heard his psychologist voice chastise him for using the word 'always.' Things were rarely *always* or *never* and he'd fallen into the trap.

"I'm just being honest. This isn't about me."

Ben's mouth tightened. The more he tried to back off, the more his anger refused to cool. "It's always about you, and it always has been." Dammit, there was the word again. Twice. He forced himself to, literally, bite his tongue.

Raven slammed the trunk lid down, breathing hard, and shook her fist at him. "You are not taking my son away. Ever." Her eyes practically flamed.

Ben took a step back and breathed a long, slow breath. "Raven, what's really going on here? Something's bothering you a whole lot more than the idea of sending the kids here to spend the holidays with me and Julie."

"It's … never mind. I'll work it out, not any of your business."

"If it concerns Zac, it damn sure is my business." He took a step forward and reached for her hand, but the timing was off. She pulled her arm back, then lashed out and swung the duffle, catching him on the chin.

He held up both hands, surrendering. "Okay, okay. We're both tired from our travels and we'll need to discuss this later, when we can both be more rational, less emotional."

She spun on her heel and stomped back toward the hotel entrance. Ben let her go. Who knew when she would come around enough for a rational discussion on this subject. When, or *if*. He felt frustration well up in his chest, a strange desire to either punch something or cry.

It wasn't merely the fatigue. It was everything. The hurricane that had destroyed their home and many of their possessions, the new job, the travel, the push and pull of family decisions that never seemed to find balance. "This isn't helping." he muttered to the empty parking lot.

Ben leaned against the U-Haul truck and shut his eyes against the aftermath of the fight. He didn't need to guess what Raven's anger meant. The argument was unresolved, and she never let him have the last word for long. They'd been here before, but it never made things any easier.

He stood and walked back into the lobby. Down a corridor, before the elevators, a wide doorway led to a courtyard. Soft lighting surrounded groupings of tables and chairs, and a water feature splashed at one end of the pleasant space. Two couples occupied one of the tables, wine glasses in hand.

Ben strolled past them, forcing himself to slow down, to regroup. If the question about the holidays couldn't be solved in a cordial manner, well … he'd have to decide how hard to push. But tonight was not at all the time to make decisions like that. More than anything, he needed sleep. It was normally true, what his adopted dad used to say. Things will look different in the morning.

After a long moment, he turned back toward the elevators and rode to the third floor. He let the silence settle around him like an uneasy truce, his thoughts heavy, knowing that this wasn't over. Not by a long shot.

The moment he opened the door to their room, he realized Julie was up. Lights were on, and she sat at the table in the corner, her laptop open.

"Hey," she said.

"Hey. Sorry if I woke you."

She shook her head. "It's this story. It's not quite there yet, so I told my editor I needed a few more hours."

Yeah, right. "I didn't mean to worry you. Raven texted—"

"Trouble?"

"Same old, same old. She wasn't happy about our suggestion for the holidays, but you know. There was no reasoning with her, and I'm too tired to think about it right now." He left out the part about the raised voices and the depth of Raven's anger. His own, as well. They both needed to cool off. He only hoped the next week wouldn't be a disaster.

Chapter 7

The next day saw Ben and Julie up at dawn. They'd already discussed what to do with their full U-Haul truck, while they drove to the pueblo for the day. Leaving it in the hotel parking lot was not an option. Too many traveling families had discovered, the hard way, what a prime target these things were for thieves. It was the main reason they'd chosen a hotel that was not adjacent to an entry ramp on the interstate, one that boasted of parking lot security cameras and patrols. But now that they were checking out, they had to deal with the truck themselves.

Julie had found the best arrangement (of course she did) by coordinating with the manager of their new apartment building. The manager's brother owned a fenced and gated self storage unit and had agreed to let them park within the fence for as long as they needed to.

Loading their overnight bags into the back of her rental, Julie followed Ben and the truck. The early morning traffic was light, the manager met them right on time, and they'd soon secured the truck within the enclosure. It would only be one or two days. Both Ben and Julie were eager to get moved into the apartment where they would settle while they looked for a home to buy. And Julie had been scouring Zillow listings for the last three weeks.

Back at the hotel thirty minutes later, they spotted Raven and the boys in the restaurant, where both teens were scarfing down huge plates of pancakes.

Zac saw them and waved both arms. "Dad! Over here!"

Ben watched the tight smile on Raven's face. She didn't say anything, so he addressed the boys instead. "You guys got your stuff packed?"

"I could sure use some of those pancakes," Julie piped up, sending him a sideways look. They'd already discussed arrival time at the pueblo and didn't want to get there too early. Aunt Zena was a known early riser, but she had her set of routines before she wanted company getting in her way, especially on an occasion like this. He suspected she'd invited half the pueblo for their welcome dinner.

Raven remained quiet while the rest of them ate, her eyes mostly on her phone, even when Julie tried to engage her in conversation. Twenty minutes later, tummies full, they headed for the cars while Ben picked up the breakfast check.

Outside, Julie clicked the trunk of her rental closed and turned. "Do we have everything?" she asked.

Ben nodded. "We're packed tighter than the studio apartments you lived in back east." He smiled at her, hoping his attempt at humor was well received.

Zac and Nathan stood in the empty space where the

U-Haul had been parked, Raven's car on one side and Julie's on the other.

"I want to ride with Dad," Zac announced. He moved toward the white compact car, decision made.

Ben eyed Raven. "That's fine with us."

But Nathan noticed Raven's scowl. "Good. More room for me with Raven." Always the peacemaker in the family, this kid. He moved toward the other car, making a face at his brother as he walked.

"I guess we're set," Raven said, slipping her phone into a pocket in her fleece jacket. "I'll follow, since I don't know exactly where we're going."

Zac tossed his pack into the backseat and climbed in after it. His excitement was almost infectious.

"Got enough space back there, buddy?" Ben asked.

Julie opened the front passenger side door, stretching her arms above her head, releasing a breath she'd been holding too long. "I can't believe I finally sent that story off," she said. Her voice was lighter, as if releasing the tension that had kept her on edge the past few weeks.

Ben slid into the driver's seat, adjusting to the rented sedan's unfamiliar feel. "You did it. Finished before we hit the road," he said, starting the engine with a smooth purr.

"It could mean great things for my job prospects, look good on my resumé," Julie said as she settled in next to him, her eyes scanning his face.

"It could," Ben replied. "I hope you get the career boost you've been working so hard for."

Ben pulled out of the hotel lot, heading north on Rio Grande Boulevard. It was a scenic, almost rural part of the city and an easy connection with Alameda and a back way through Bernalillo, where they would join the highway toward Tewa. His eyes kept darting to the mirrors, making certain not to lose Raven and Nathan at one of the traffic lights.

Within twenty minutes, the landscape opened up to reveal a sweep of open desert. Ben felt the familiar call of the land, pulling at something deep within him. Julie sat back, relaxing as she thumbed through messages on her phone.

"I hope my editor doesn't call with more changes," she said, half to herself, her voice now tinged with a vulnerability she rarely showed.

"You worry too much. It's going to be great," Ben said, trying to reassure her, recalling that even finished work could require edits before it was truly done.

Julie laughed softly. "You know I always expect something to need fixing," she said. "Occupational hazard."

Ben focused on the road, negotiating traffic through Rio Rancho and Bernalillo, two small towns that had ballooned in size in recent years. Soon, the cityscape of Albuquerque began to fade behind them, replaced by the vastness of the high desert. "Just enjoy the ride for a while," he said, realizing that this trip was a crossing, a bridge between the different parts of his life.

Zac leaned forward from the back seat. "Are we almost there?" he joked, his eyes sparkling with mischief. This lanky stretch of adolescence gave him a confidence that was both endearing and bittersweet to Ben.

"Not quite, kiddo. Another hour or so," Ben replied, smiling at his son. "Excited?"

"Yep. I can't wait to see everything. I barely remember it from the first time." Zac buzzed with enthusiasm.

Ben felt a surge of affection. "You might end up

wanting to stay longer than we planned," he said, half teasing, half serious.

Julie turned to look at Zac, her face softening with warmth. "You're going to love it," she said.

Ben glanced in the mirror, seeing Raven's car about a half-mile behind. "Zac, I noticed your mom seems a bit … I don't know … preoccupied."

"Grumpy."

"What's going on? She got something on her mind that she hasn't told me?"

"I dunno. She's been like this for a few weeks now. I heard her saying something to Uncle E.J. about making a change."

"What kind of change?" Ben pictured that there might be a boyfriend. Raven was still a stunningly beautiful woman.

Zac leaned forward between the two front seats. "I think it's got something to do with her shop. Like maybe it's not doing so well. Money's been a sore subject."

And yet, Raven hadn't allowed him to cover her expenses for this trip or accepted his offer for more than his usual monthly amount for the boys' support. Ben pondered that.

"Surely tattoos aren't going out of fashion anytime soon," Julie mused, her eyes still on her messages.

Zac's mouth gave a twist. "People seem to always be coming in there, so that doesn't make sense. All I know is, she won't do one for me until I turn eighteen. At least that's what she says. I have this idea for a cool one."

"On that subject, I have to agree with your mother," Ben said, smiling quickly at his son. "Eighteen is still pretty young to make a lifetime decision."

His thoughts drifted to the significance of this trip, returning to the pueblo where he'd spent childhood summers, weaving between worlds. It felt like it would be more than a quick visit.

"What's going on inside that handsome head of yours?" Julie teased.

"Memories. The summers at the pueblo were so rich and vibrant. The feel of sunbaked earth under my bare feet, the night sky so dark we could lie on our backs and see a zillion stars all at once, the bright fields of corn and squash. The rhythms of community life, the laughter, me and my cousins playing in the dirt, the soft Tewa words of my grandmother teaching me the old ways. Such a sense of belonging and freedom, where we kids moved through the world with unburdened hearts." He paused a moment and swallowed hard.

"There were ceremonies in the kiva," he continued, "times when the entire Pueblo seemed to hum with life and connection. Those summers gave me a foundation, a sense of self rooted in tradition and family. They've always been a part of me, even when the distance seemed too great. Funny how vivid those memories are, even though I was only five when my mother died. And it wasn't long before my grandmother decided I should have the advantages of a white upbringing."

Julie reached for his hand. "That must have been … well, different."

"A contrast, for sure. In Utah everything felt foreign and strange. I remember the awkwardness of standing out, the tall Indian boy in a classroom full of white faces. The lessons I learned there were valuable in their own way, teaching me resilience, adaptability, the ability to navigate unfamiliar waters. My grandmother's decision to send me away was difficult, but it was made from love and foresight. I knew that even at the time. It gave me opportunities, opened doors I might never have experienced had I stayed with her. A college education and the chance to become a doctor who could help Indian people—I wouldn't have traded that for anything. I guess I always walked the line between two worlds, never fully in one or the other."

"I'm glad we're doing this together," Julie said.

The highway stretched out before them, through the high desert. The landscape opened wide, horizons blurring into the surrounding foothills under the cobalt sky. Ben's eyes scanned the mirrors frequently, making sure the rest of their short caravan was still back there. He would try to find a chance to ask Raven about what Zac had said, if things were okay at her tattoo shop.

"You look serious," Julie teased, glancing over with a knowing smile. "Regretting not packing more boxes?"

Ben smirked, keeping his eyes on the road. "Just trying to remember the first time you took this trip with me." He paused, the memories as vivid as the reddish earth around them. "You were more of a New York career girl back then."

"And you're still a puzzle," she replied. "But I like puzzles." Her hand brushed his shoulder, grounding him with her presence.

Zac's voice broke in. "Hey, is that one of those dirt tornadoes?" he asked, his excitement palpable as he pointed to a swirl of dust twirling across the horizon.

"A dust devil!" Ben answered, glad for the distraction. "Keep your eyes peeled and you might see a few more."

Julie leaned back, giving Zac a conspiratorial wink.

"Better than video games, right?"

"Way better," Zac declared, his attention jumping from one sight to the next like a grasshopper. He snapped pictures on his phone, the clicks punctuating his fascination. His ability to embrace new experiences reminded Ben of his own youthful summers—although Zac had the continuity of family on Raven's side, something Ben had once longed for.

He caught sight of the other vehicle in the rearview mirror, its white sparkle catching the sun. Raven and Nathan were still back there, the distance between them closing. He imagined Raven's focused eyes, Nathan's youthful enthusiasm echoing Zac's. He was glad they had left together from Albuquerque, and she had stuck with their agreement to keep pace on the drive to the pueblo.

"Looks like the caravan's sticking together," Julie observed, following his gaze.

Ben nodded, refocusing on the road ahead, noticing the upcoming curves in the ribbon of highway disappearing into the horizon. It had been years since he'd driven this stretch, but now he remembered the sign—a yellow warning with black slashes—before his mind registered its gravity. Dangerous curves. He should have remembered to warn Raven. And now her car was speeding up behind him, even as he hit the brakes.

Chapter 8

He concentrated on steering safely through the curve, his mouth frozen in a grimace. Only when the road straightened again did he dare look back in the mirror.

Nothing.

He slowed and let the car coast along, watching continuously for the other vehicle to come into sight. It didn't. Uttering a soft curse, he pulled over to the shoulder, dread lying heavy in his gut.

"Ben?" Julie's face was too pale.

He shook his head. Zac sat in the back seat, earbuds plugged in, and now he looked up. "Why'd we stop?"

"I need to check on something," Ben told them, his calm, professional voice belying what was going on in his head.

He made a U-turn and drove slowly back to the curve.

The broken guardrail said it all. And now he remembered the steep drop-off below, where the cruelty of physics would have pulled at the speeding car behind him, carrying it out of sight below.

Another vehicle had stopped alongside the northbound lane. For a split second he hoped it was Raven's car. But this one was red, a pickup truck.

He pulled as far off the road as he could get, given the narrow confines of the curve, wrenched open the door, and shouted toward the driver of the red truck. "Did you see—?"

The man, Tewa by the look of him, wearing a plaid shirt and Levi's, simply pointed downward toward the chasm.

"Julie, call for help," Ben gasped, her name coming out more a huff than a word. He reached inside and switched on his emergency flashers. Other cars began to catch up, their drivers slowing to gawk.

Julie was already moving, phone in hand, her instincts from years of crisis reporting snapping into place. In mere seconds she'd phoned for help, her voice steady and clipped even as she imparted the terrible news. "Be careful, Ben," she said, one foot out of the car, eyes fixed on the chaos around them.

"Stay here, Zac!" Ben yelled as he stepped away from the rental car. It was more command than request, a shield to keep his son from seeing what they already knew: The crash was surely merciless.

Ben checked both directions before dashing across the two-lane highway. The man from the red truck was standing at the edge of the precipice and Ben joined him. Five hundred feet below lay the mangled fragments of a white car.

"They take the curve too fast," the stranger said. "It is not the first time." He shook his head sadly and walked back to his truck.

By this time, at least six other vehicles had come to a stop, while a few others cautiously edged their way through the melee. Ben realized the emergency vehicles would never get through if everyone else blocked the narrow road. He stepped to the middle and began waving the onlookers through.

"Keep it moving, folks. We need to let the police get in." At this moment he wasn't sure whether they were on state land or pueblo land. And he supposed it didn't matter. He kept waving cars through until he heard sirens approaching from both directions.

As he walked back to Julie and Zac in the rental car, he had a horrible thought. Raven's surly moods, problems with her business or who-knew-what-else—could she have had a suicide wish? No! She had Nathan with her. Would have had Zac with her, if their son hadn't insisted on riding in the other car.

But still, Ben swore she was speeding up as he slowed, going into the curve.

* * *

The highway became a chaotic hive as emergency vehicles swarmed the scene. Police lights stung the air, painting everything with garish reds and blues. Ben stood rooted in disbelief, his sense of time and place slipping. Only when an officer approached and asked him to move along, did he find the energy to respond. "They're family. My other son is in that vehicle!"

Zac crossed the road, dodging between two moving vehicles, and an officer grabbed him. "You can't go over there, son. Come on, wait with your folks."

The cop led them back to the rental car and told everyone to wait, to keep out of the way. Julie pulled Zac into a hug, meeting Ben's stunned gaze over the boy's shoulder, tears running down her face.

More police arrived, directing traffic single file through the scene, making the northbound and southbound lanes take turns. It became a nightmare circus, too much flashing light, too real. An ambulance arrived, pulling into the spot where the red pickup truck had been. The old man must have followed orders and left the scene. Ben wanted to thank him for stopping but doubted he would ever get the chance.

EMTs and a rescue team approached the cliff's edge, some sliding down the embankment to reach the mangled vehicle below. Shouts came from below, incomprehensible sounds that pounded against Ben's skull.

He saw a female officer glance his way, a grim look of understanding passing between them, a slight shake of the head that confirmed the worst. Ben couldn't move, couldn't respond. The full weight of the moment crushed his chest, making it hard to breathe. Raven. Nathan. Gone. It felt like the world had shifted on its axis, leaving him unmoored.

Julie was with Zac now, crouching beside where he sat near the back door of the car, wrapping him in a blanket that an EMT handed over. "I've got you," she murmured to Zac, but Ben knew those words were meant for him too.

Zac's eyes were wide and glassy, darting between Ben and Julie, struggling to make sense of it all. "Mom?

Nathan? Can the rescue guys reach them?"

"I don't know, buddy," Ben said, his own voice raw, stripped bare. But he did know. He knew he couldn't let his son witness the carnage. He sank to his knees beside them, the gravel biting his skin. The sensation grounded him enough to stay present.

Julie enveloped them both, her touch gentle and sure. "We're together," she whispered, a promise and a plea. Ben still couldn't quite process the enormity of the loss. How would Zac deal with it?

A state police helicopter arrived, circling, then hovering in front of the cliffside. The female officer approached, drawing Ben aside, keeping her voice low. "I understand the vehicle belonged to some of your family?"

He stared toward the rescuers, nodding vacantly. As she asked questions and took notes, he answered numbly. Names, home address, next of kin.

"So, all of you were headed to Tewa Pueblo this morning? You have more family there?"

He ran a hand across his forehead. "Yes, my extended family. Raven's from Alaska, well, recently living in Washington state. We ..." His voice petered out as his thoughts became a jumble. There were too many people to notify, too many logistics to think about right now.

Another officer, an older man, approached and the two law enforcement people stepped aside and conferred quietly. Ben noticed they represented both state and tribal police. The woman who'd interviewed him walked back.

"It's going to take a while for us to, um, finish up here. The bodies will be taken to Albuquerque, to the Office of the Medical Investigator, for autopsy. It's standard. My colleague and I think it would be best that you and your wife and son not hang around for that. You don't want the boy seeing them in their … condition."

Ben's throat tightened.

"Since you have other family at Tewa, you might want to go along there. Families need support at times like this."

He wanted to tell her he was a psychologist, he knew about finding support in times of trauma. But he'd never experienced this much shock, up close and personal. He finally managed to nod and turn back toward Julie and Zac.

Julie was holding it together, only just, for Zac's sake. Someone had given him a bottle of water and a candy bar. She gave Zac's shoulder a squeeze, then turned to Ben. "We'll figure this out," she said, and though her voice was steady, her eyes betrayed the shock they all felt.

Ben's thoughts were jagged and disordered, but he had to pull himself together and get them to the safety of the pueblo, away from the chaos and the relentless sound of the helicopter's blades.

He got behind the wheel, took a breath, told Julie and Zac to buckle up. As he turned the rental car back in the direction of Tewa, he knew this was only the beginning.

Chapter 9

Ben noticed the trees as the car rolled into Tewa Pueblo. A strange thing to focus on at a time like this, he thought, the fact that the cottonwoods and elms were beginning to show the first faint yellow signs of autumn. The tires whispered over the dirt road, stirring up a cloud of memories.

Familiar buildings clustered together, one home built against the side of another, in the traditional way that never changed. The kiva rose against a vast sky, forming a backdrop for his nostalgia and grief to intermingle. He glanced at Zac and Julie; their eyes reflected the same heaviness he felt. When he stopped the car in front of his childhood home, they all hesitated, as though stepping out meant accepting their unspeakable loss. Then he opened the door.

Ben was first to get out, his track shoes shuffling on the packed earth. He looked around, eyes sweeping over the adobe houses with their smooth walls and chimney stacks. The world felt different and too familiar, all at once. Zac followed, standing close to Ben, lost in his own quiet thoughts. Julie took her time, gathering her purse, holding back so Ben could wrap a comforting arm around Zac's shoulders. They moved as a unit toward the house, the pull of family and the reality of the tragedy surrounding them.

His relatives emerged, one by one, the aunts and uncles Ben hadn't seen in far too long. Their voices mingled in a soft chorus of grief and welcome. Apparently, Elmore Waquie, the longtime chief of police here at the pueblo, had already delivered the news of the accident. The aunts enveloped Ben in embraces then moved to Zac, wrapping him in the same gentle care, murmuring soft Tewa words that reached him even when language could not. It was family at its rawest—knowing, hurting, and holding together.

Ben marveled at how the faces had changed during the years he'd been away—showing new creases in the skin, more gray in the dark hair—but the old bonds were unbroken. Looking at his extended family was like looking at a photograph missing its center, his grandmother's absence reminding him of another, older loss. He let the family voices draw him back, their hands gentle on his shoulders, their presence a much-needed salve. The warmth of kinship extended, wrapping around Zac and Julie, holding them together.

As they entered his grandmother's house, which her daughter Zena had taken over, Ben felt the adobe walls and packed dirt floors, exactly as he remembered from childhood. Each piece of traditional pottery and every woven rug meant a specific thing from his past, things he recalled even during the years he'd lived away. His totem, a small opossum skull he'd found as a child, still sat on the mantle. He drew comfort from the unchanging nature of life here.

Julie walked beside him and reached for his hand. He glanced at Zac, who silently took in the scene with wide eyes, absorbing the culture he'd never fully experienced during his too-few, too-short visits.

Zac's perspective added another layer to Ben's own. While Ben saw his history in every corner of the room, he knew Zac was seeing an unfamiliar heritage, far from his own Native Alaskan upbringing. Being here at the pueblo was supposed to be a chance for them all to connect more deeply with this side of their lives, but the accident had painted over everything with shock and disbelief. Raven had been such a small part of Ben's life, in everyday terms, but a huge part as well, as the mother of his child. He felt a momentary surge of fury toward his ex-girlfriend. Then he tamped it down, knowing full well that anger was also a part of the grieving process.

He turned his attention to his immediate surroundings. Aunt Zena, his mother's sister, stepped forward and placed her palms on the sides of Ben's face. A soft endearment in Tewa, a sad smile. Ben wished he could recall the words he'd long forgotten, but it was her presence, the caring that meant everything. The memory of his mother returned full-force, even though he'd only been five when she died.

Randomly, he wondered if Nia would have found better help for her problems if she'd lived. Alcoholism was more treatable, less accepted as a matter of fate within the community, now than it had been forty-some years ago.

He swallowed back those thoughts and bent to kiss Zena's cheek.

His aunt looked so much like he imagined his mother would look today, and her artistic nature was clear in every room of the house, from the bundles of dried flowers on the kitchen walls to the pottery above the fireplace in the living room.

"Come," she said, "sit down. I have chile stew on the stove, and the others are bringing tortillas, beans, and that special cornbread you love so much."

Indeed, the women in the group seemed to have vanished, disappearing to other rooms and to their own homes. And if Ben knew them by their traditions, each would have been cooking all morning to assemble the meal for the visitors.

"Hey, Zac," he said, wanting to tousle his son's hair but refraining. Seventeen wasn't the age when kids welcomed that stuff. Zac wasn't ten anymore. "See if you can help by bringing in some extra firewood."

His son gave him a stony look, until Julie gently reminded that the kitchen stove was an ancient wood-burner and the night would be chilly enough for the fireplace. Without a word, Zac followed one of the cousins, a kid about the same age whose name Ben couldn't readily recall, and the two went outside toward the woodpile.

"It hasn't hit him yet," Ben told Zena.

She nodded. "Might take a while. Patience is needed."

A sound at the front door caught his attention. Through the open doorway, his cousin Vicente entered. For an instant, Ben was ten years old again, Vicente fourteen, and the memory of the time his teenage cousin was trusted to drive Uncle's decrepit pickup truck. The thing was a fossil. Peeling paint, bald patches across the hood, one back fender missing, the front two mismatched in color, and smooth tires without a speck of tread. The tailgate was wired shut and it surely had no license plate.

After the boys had picked corn for half a day, Vicente was instructed to drive back down to the village, unload the pickings, and get more sacks while Ben and his uncle waited at the cornfield. And on the way down the hill, he misjudged a curve and rolled the old truck, suffering a broken arm. Ben felt his breath catch. The similarity made his chest contract.

"Seems you had a new family I didn't know about," Vicente said, his tone light but with its usual edge. There'd almost always been friction between them. Three of the other men edged out through the open door.

Ben blinked, forcing his voice to remain calm. "Raven was someone I knew a long time ago. Nathan was Zac's best friend. His adopted brother." The words sounded distant even to his own ears.

"You seem to have a knack for adopting family, don't you, Benson?" Vicente's voice gave challenge, disguised as curiosity.

"I guess I do. And now we're reconnecting," Ben replied, maintaining his composure. "That's why we're here."

Aunt Dora stepped past her son. "We're glad you're here, Ben. It's good to see you after so long. And to have another nephew," she added when Zac walked in with an armload of split logs. Julie had disappeared into the kitchen with an offer to help set the table.

Vicente's skepticism was evident as he leaned on the doorjamb, arms crossed. "So, is this a quick visit, or are you sticking around this time?"

Ben felt a familiar tension but chose his words with care. "I'll be working with the Indian Health Service in Albuquerque. We plan to spend as much time here as we can."

Vicente leaned forward, his eyes narrowing slightly. "What about all that other stuff you do? You know, the white man's world?" His words hung in the air, daring a response.

Ben paused, sensing the family's attention. "It's part of who I am. But so is the pueblo." He tried to bridge the gap, but Vicente's smirk suggested a widening chasm instead.

The exchange pulled at Ben, his professional tone clashing with the rawness of their history as boys, the fact that Vicente had been the bully in the group. With Ben's half-Anglo features and his years in Utah, he was an outsider in his cousin's opinion. And despite Ben's professional experience, Vicente had a way of piercing his shield, bringing back his old insecurities.

Zac, sensing the crackling tension, broke the quiet with a question. "Tell me more about the harvest festival." His eyes flicked between Vicente and Ben, searching for an anchor in the shifting emotions.

Ben recognized the effort, the way Zac tried to steer them toward common ground, in the same way he'd diffused tensions with Raven. The family's attention shifted to the younger voice, the reminder of a new generation and the ties that bound them, however tenuous. They were all dealing with loss right now, and he wanted to be there for all of them.

Vicente's expression softened, his focus turning to Zac. "Sure, kid."

Ben watched the room ease, Vicente might be a jerk at times, but his response showed a sign of pride in traditions handed down.

Zac shifted on his feet, not sure of Vicente's offer, but ready to claim it. And although his eyes were still haunted, the grief receded a tiny bit as the boy listened, moving between cultures with a fluidity Ben both admired and envied. During his summers here, he recalled his own struggle to fit in, the whispered worries from the elders, that he would forget this life, punctuated by the taunts of Vicente and a couple of the older cousins.

"Is there really a custom with snakes?" Zac's question cut through, his eyes wide. "Do they bite?"

Vicente relaxed, his voice proud. "Not if you know how to handle them."

Ben shot his cousin a look. None of the pueblos used live snakes in any ceremony he knew about.

"Okay, okay, I'm pulling your leg. That's a Hopi thing," Vicente admitted. "No ceremonial snakes at Tewa, but you might run across a rattler if you go hiking around out here. And their bite can be deadly. Be careful not to place your hands or feet somewhere you can't see."

"That's great advice, Zac," Ben added. "It's exactly what the elders taught us as kids."

"All right, everyone. Dinner is ready," Dora called from the kitchen doorway.

The women stood aside as the men shuffled forward, moving past the hot stovetop to accept bowls of the stew and beans, a tortilla or a square of the cornbread plopped on top of it.

"Take a place at the table or go on out the back door and find seats on the portal," Zena instructed as she ladled stew for everyone.

The scent of the meat and chile stew rose from their ceramic bowls, sending up waves of comfort and familiarity. Ben saw Zac head out back with some other kids about his age. He watched for Julie and made sure she caught his eye. As his family gathered, soft laughter and voices swelled into a warm, living backdrop. The tasty food, rich with history and flavor, briefly obscured the raw sense of loss.

Ben found a seat near Uncle Joe, keeping an eye on Zac whose group had settled at the far end of the portal, separate from the adults. He watched Zac's expressions ebb and flow, between the shock of the day's events and the stories going on around him, as he listened to the cousins go on about their summer chores, tending the fields of corn, beans, and squash. When someone asked, he shared that he raised sled dogs and was involved with the Iditarod. It was a balm to see his son interacting in this unfamiliar world.

Julie walked out and sat near him, sitting cross-legged on the wooden planks and balancing her dish on her lap. While he ate, Ben sensed a loosening of the day's tensions, though an undercurrent of sadness still wove through the moment.

As dinner ended, Ben watched family members gather the dishes, their movements as coordinated as a well-rehearsed play. One of the teenage girls came around to collect their bowls, declining his offer to help with the dishes. "Next time. Tonight, you are the guest."

Nonetheless, he picked up a few plates and bowls and carried them into the kitchen. Teens and young mothers seemed to be in charge of kitchen cleanup. The older women had retired from their cooking duties and were relaxing in the living room in front of the cozy kiva fireplace.

Ben stepped outside, where the pueblo's nighttime sounds greeted him—distant voices, a coyote's call, the wind threading through bare branches. He spotted Julie at the trunk of the rental car, digging for a jacket.

"Guess my blood thinned, living in the tropics," she teased, slipping her arms into the soft fleece.

"Should I take one for Zac?" he wondered.

"Don't worry about him. He'll come and find his when he needs it. Don't forget, he's been in the Pacific Northwest or Alaska all his life. He's acclimated." She stepped over to face Ben and slip her arms around his neck. "Are you okay?"

He nodded. "As okay as I can be. I keep thinking that I should reach out to Nathan's people. I know the police were going to notify the Navajo tribal authority, but …"

"This also requires the Pecos personal touch. Sometime in the next few days will be fine, I'm sure."

He nodded agreement. "Were you thinking we would drive back to Albuquerque tonight? It's only about ninety minutes."

"Your Aunt Zena offered us beds here." She checked the locks on the car doors, out of habit. "I don't know about you, but I'm beat. And our apartment has nothing at all ready for move-in."

They'd rented a furnished place, planning only to unpack kitchen gear and Julie's office equipment. It was a temporary home until they bought a house. And hadn't their insurance agent said the settlement check for their hurricane losses should be coming through nearly any day now?

Ben smiled down at her. "You're right. We're both too tired to drive. Tell Zena we accept, gratefully. And ask her if there's anything I can do to get things ready."

Julie gave his hand a gentle squeeze and walked back toward the house, where it appeared the extended family were taking their leave, most of them walking a few doors away to their own homes. Ben strolled back and settled onto the porch, trying a meditation technique to make the day's tensions quit gnawing at him. Moments later, Vicente joined him, his presence subtly shifting the air.

They sat in silence at first. Ben felt the temperature contrast to the afternoon's warmth and a reminder that temperatures in the high desert normally dropped by twenty degrees after sundown. He finally spoke, needing to share his thoughts. "Even though I'll be working out of Albuquerque, I want you to know we plan on staying here a lot. It's important for me to be connected to this place." He paused, gauging Vicente's reaction. "For Zac, too."

Vicente couldn't quite mask his skepticism. "And you think you can do that? Live here and there, like it's no big deal?"

Ben took a moment, letting the question settle. "It's not always been easy," he admitted. "But Julie and I agree that this move feels right."

Vicente leaned back, his body language softening slightly. "You seem more sure of it than before," he said, though his tone suggested he wasn't convinced.

"I am," Ben replied. The assurance in his voice came from a place he was still learning to trust. "I can't change where I've been or how I got here. But I can be here now."

Vicente turned his gaze to the darkened landscape, the distant mesas outlined against the moonlit sky. "It was never easy, even for those of us who stayed. There's a lot to live up to."

Ben heard the echo of his own struggles in Vicente's words. The recognition wove a tenuous thread between them, the vague possibility of understanding.

"It's hard for everyone," Ben offered. "In different ways."

The silence between them felt less like tension and more like an opening, though it was clear the divide still lingered. The fragility of their bond was apparent, yet so was the potential for the paths that branched between them to be not as separate as he'd once thought. Eventually, Vicente stood up, groaning slightly with the effort, giving a grunted goodnight.

Ben stood and stretched, walked out into the open under the vast, star-speckled sky, the cool night needling his skin. The events of the day clung to him. The image of the mangled car felt both surreal and raw, a sight burned into his brain.

The weird nature of Raven's accident nagged at him, disbelief interwoven with the fresh pang of mourning. She and Nathan were supposed to be here, a vital piece of this reunion, and their absence was as palpable as their presence would have been. The morning's conflict and confusion meshed with loss; he should have known exactly how to deal with it but he didn't.

Yet, he found threads of solace in his family's support. The gathering had wrapped around them like one of his grandmother's handmade blankets, affirming connections that transcended loss. Gratitude filled him, leaving Ben both comforted and restless, the enormity of it all pulling at the seams of his composure.

He knew the calm would give way, the surface peace

disrupted. Grieving was not a straightforward process; he and Zac were only at the beginning. For now, the embrace of family held him steady. He was profoundly thankful for that.

Chapter 10

Julie kept him talking during the drive back to the city the following morning. Ben noticed that she hardly slowed as they passed the accident scene, a spot along the highway where no one would know death had occurred, if not for the broken guardrail. It felt a bit disrespectful, but he knew the reason—neither of them wanted Zac to relive the traumatic day quite this soon.

Ben would have suggested taking an alternate route, but roads through tribal lands were few and far between and any other way would have added close to three hours to the trip. As it was, they were anxious to get their things unloaded at their Albuquerque apartment and the U-Haul truck returned. Distractions, at this point, were welcome.

"So, cars. What do you think?" Julie's question pulled him back to the other somewhat urgent item on their agenda. They didn't want to keep paying a daily rate on the rental, and Ben would need a vehicle by next week in order to start his new job.

"Something with great fuel efficiency would be smart," he said. "But I'm thinking a pickup or high-clearance SUV will be a must for me, roads in and out of the pueblos can be rough and especially dicey if there's heavy rain."

Zac stared out at the cloudless sky. "Heavy rain? Does that happen?"

"Not often enough. Which is why it's a problem when it does." He remembered his grandmother's tales of flash floods and rushing to higher ground on several occasions.

Traffic increased as they reached the northern edge of Albuquerque, but Julie handled it like a pro. She exited at San Mateo, blended into the crowded lanes on Academy, and pulled into the storage place where they'd left the U-Haul.

Fifteen minutes later, the two vehicles were parked in front of their new apartment, the truck with its back door open and ramp in place. While Ben and Zac wheeled a dolly back and forth with boxes, Julie ran an efficient relay, setting out what they would need in the immediate future and stacking everything else wherever it would fit—along the bedroom walls, in closets, under the dining table.

"I'm beginning to think we were lucky that most of our possessions did *not* survive the hurricane," she told Ben as he announced this was the last load. "We would have filled a full-sized moving van."

He glanced into the smaller of the two bedrooms, where Zac was making his bed with sheets Julie had left out for him. "We may still need to rent some storage. I have no idea how much stuff he has, back at Raven's house."

The reminder sent a shadow over the room.

"We'll figure it out," Julie assured him. "For now, I'd better follow you over to the U-Haul place and give you a ride back."

* * *

By two p.m. they'd made significant progress. A quick grocery stop after dropping off the truck had netted enough supplies for simple breakfasts and lunches, and Ben had put together some sandwiches while Julie browsed real estate listings online.

"If you boys don't mind organizing our kitchen gear," she said, "I'll see if I can get some appointments set up. The sooner we find a permanent home, the sooner we can quit living out of boxes."

Zac pulled the cartons marked "Kitchen" and Ben began putting pots, pans, dishes, and utensils in the cupboards. "I hope everyone can find what they need," he said, stuffing a spatula, two wooden spoons, the potato masher, and salad tongs into the ceramic container they'd used for the same purpose before.

"Honey, what do you think about this place?" Julie asked, drawing his attention to the dining table where she'd set up her makeshift research desk.

She turned her laptop screen to face him, revealing a white stucco house with red tile roof, archways above the doors and windows, and tall shade trees in the yard.

"Looks like an older neighborhood, which we always love," he said. "Three bedrooms are perfect, but don't you think it's above our budget?"

She nodded. Their insurance settlement would only go so far, and with Julie now unemployed, they would need to plan wisely. "I'm calling the agent. Maybe the owner is willing to negotiate."

Ben wandered into Zac's bedroom to see how his son was settling in. It felt like less than five minutes later when Julie popped her head in at the doorway. "We have an appointment to meet the Realtor there at three-thirty, and it's clear across town from here. You guys ready to head out?"

They pulled up to the curb at the house on Sixteenth Street, a neighborhood of older homes, bungalows and ranch style, not far from Old Town. The real estate agent got out of her shiny pearl-white Lexus, put on her best smile, and approached with her hand extended as she introduced herself as Amy Lang.

They followed her inside and loved what they saw. Original hardwood floors, hand-smoothed adobe interior walls, a modernized kitchen and bathroom, and three spacious bedrooms. "Newer homes aren't like this," Amy said, pointing out the size of the rooms and mature plantings in the back yard.

When Ben asked if the price was negotiable, unfortunately, the answer was negative. Amy tried to make the best of it. "It's only been on the market a week, and the seller is fairly confident of getting a full-price offer. With today's market, I think they're right."

She noticed their disappointment.

Julie had pulled out her phone and scrolled to some other listings.

"I do have another possible option," Amy said, "although I hesitate to show it right now. It has everything you love about this one—older home in an established neighborhood, only four blocks from here. But it was owned by an elderly couple, husband recently passed and Mom has moved in with her daughter. The kids—in their sixties—have taken over trying to help her out, and the place is now in the middle of having upgrades and renovations done. It isn't officially listed yet."

"Can you show us?" Julie immediately put away her phone.

Amy nodded. "I will warn you, we'd be walking into a construction zone."

"We just moved out of a hurricane area. I think we can handle it," Ben said with a smile.

* * *

Ben walked through the house, catching glimpses of the late-afternoon sky through the windows. The vivid clouds felt like an old friend. He took a moment to savor it, appreciating the uniquely New Mexico touches.

"This place is huge compared to the old one," Zac remarked, trailing behind him.

"Plenty of room to spread out," Ben agreed. "A bit different, right?"

"A lot different," Zac said, his voice slightly awed. "Kinda cool, though."

Ben watched his son wander to the window, observing the park-like surroundings and the Sandia Mountains in the distance. It was a striking change from the palm trees and the smell of the ocean. Or from the pueblo, where the high desert mountains loomed close and familiar.

Julie turned in circles, imagining how each room would look. Despite the ladders and buckets of stain in the living and dining rooms, and the kitchen being stripped to the studs, she could envision the home's potential.

"I would need to check and see if there's still time for you to make your own choices in cabinetry and appliances," Amy said. She found a folder on her phone and opened some pictures. "Here's what the sellers have chosen."

Julie was ecstatic to see that they'd gone with traditional wood with a New Mexico flair and countertops that reflected Southwestern style, not the sterile white-on-white-on-white that so many favored in recent years. She glanced at Ben, who nodded. "We love it. Can we have a minute to talk about this?"

Amy walked out to the back yard to give them some space.

"It'll be fun," Julie said, coming up behind him with a playful nudge. "I can't wait to choose our own paint colors. Zac and I will have all kinds of plans for his room." She winked at her stepson.

Amy had given them an idea of what the asking price would be, and Julie's logical brain had already latched onto it, with their budget in mind. She reached for her phone again, tapped in some numbers and began calculating what they could offer. She showed Ben the screen. "We might even offer a bit less if we say we'll take over working with the reno crew and see it through."

"Don't forget, I have a job to start on Monday," he reminded.

"But I don't. And I love doing this sort of thing." There would be at least a month, maybe two, to complete the renovations on the kitchen and two bathrooms. It would give Julie a focus outside of the tragedy while she put out feelers for employment.

They smiled at each other. He knew how her mind

worked. "Have Amy write up the offer and we'll see what happens." He was happy to see her enthusiasm. It felt infectious, pulling him away from the turmoil of recent weeks and the tragedy of the past two days.

* * *

Together, they opened boxes and moved their few pieces of furniture, a vintage dresser and a few end tables, mainly. Ben promised to get to a store and buy a TV set, sometime tomorrow. There weren't many options for where things could fit, and it wasn't long before their efforts began to pay off. As they unpacked a few personal items the apartment was transforming, taking on a personality that felt more like their own. Ben unrolled a Tewa rug onto the hard floor. The muted wool patterns, from his grandparents' house, seemed to sit uneasily in the modern apartment. But as he placed pieces of pottery and framed prints, warmth began to creep into the cold edges. Maybe, he thought, they could make it work here. Maybe Zac would settle and enjoy his final year of high school. The sweet scent of Russian olive trees from the landscape plants outside their window dominated. He could almost taste New Mexico on his tongue.

Zac flopped onto the couch that had come with the furnished apartment, staring up at the ceiling fan. "Can we get a hammock for the back patio?" he asked, already imagining the new house would be theirs.

"I think we can manage that," Ben said, considering the large outdoor space. It would be nice to sit out there in the evenings, the desert cooling around them.

"The stars will be amazing," Julie said, echoing his thoughts.

Ben wrapped his arms around her from behind, resting his chin on her shoulder. They stood near the window for a moment, watching Zac test out different spots on the couch, searching for the best angle. The tension of the move seemed to ease a bit.

"Thanks for doing this," Ben said softly, touching her chin, tilting her head to meet his eyes.

"For agreeing to the patio hammock?" she teased.

He nudged her gently. "For making this move, for jumping into a new adventure."

"It's what we do, isn't it?" she replied. "We'll make each new space ours, like we always do."

It was reassuring to hear her say it out loud. To believe it. Ben hoped all of them could embrace this move, to find happiness. He turned to stack some of the boxes out of the way.

"Can you believe how much we managed to fit in that van?" A half hour had passed and Julie stood with her fists on her hips, looking around the somewhat-less-cluttered room. Her red-gold curls caught the final light from the west-facing window. The view, Ben had to admit, was spectacular.

"I'm surprised the truck made it here at all," he replied, shaking his head as he recalled the time when a rented truck had conked out on him on the way to the Navajo rez. "That old engine seemed to struggle with the altitude. You doing okay, Zac?"

The teen gave a halfhearted grunt from his corner, where he was emptying video game cases and action figures. "Yeah, it's just weird." He looked up, his eyes moist, his dark hair flopping forward . He turned his back and changed the subject. "I mean, I didn't realize I had this much of my stuff at your place in Florida."

Ben watched his son, recognizing a touch of his own unease reflected in the seventeen-year-old's demeanor. This move was an adjustment for all of them, but Ben knew it would be toughest on Zac. Leaving Washington, losing his mom and brother so suddenly, and settling into an entirely new environment. "You wanna talk?"

Zac shook his head, not ready.

"It'll feel less weird once we're unpacked," Ben assured him, moving to open another box. "Once we have a house and get your stuff from Bellingham, when your room's set up, you'll feel more at home."

"Think of it as a chance to explore a new place. Not many people get to live in so many interesting spots." Julie's attempt to pull Zac out of his funk fell flat.

"Yeah, it's like my whole life is a tour," Zac muttered, but there was a hint of a smile. "Okay, okay, I'm getting used to it."

Ben was encouraged by the slight softening in Zac's tone. He hoped his son would find it easier once he made friends, once he found a rhythm in this new city. Albuquerque was a far cry from all of Zac's prior homes. But Ben had to admit, he was excited to see what the next phase held.

"Hey, if we get this stuff done fast, we can hit that pizza place up the street—Dion's," Ben offered. "I hear it's the best in the city."

This time the smile was genuine, and Ben felt a swell of relief. Maybe it wouldn't take long for his son to adapt, after all. "Deal. And I want root beer."

"It's good to be back in New Mexico," Julie said, more to Ben than to Zac. She had given up a national reporting job, then her position at the *Miami Herald,* for this man, truly wanting to return to where they'd met so many years ago. Now her options were open—maybe she'd take something part-time, freelancing stories she cared about, spending more time with the family. Maybe a podcast or blog would be in her future.

Ben nodded, agreeing, allowing himself to relax into her optimism. It *was* good to be back. There was a familiar comfort to the landscape. He smiled at her, then grabbed his keys, ready to check out that pizza place.

They were halfway through a medium pepperoni and mushroom, talking about how it truly was the best pizza they'd ever had, when Amy Lang phoned.

"I've got some positive news for you."

Julie let out a whoop that attracted looks from other diners. She nodded. "Yes, sure, okay," then, "See you tomorrow." She looked up at Ben and Zac, her face beaming. "Our offer was accepted, 'gratefully' Amy says. The sellers are more than happy to be done with the construction work and really happy to know we plan to live in the house and love it. They wanted to avoid selling their family home to flippers. We need to go by Amy's office tomorrow to sign the contract, and everyone's in agreement that we'll aim for a quick closing."

They tapped their soda cups together in a silly toast to the event. "Think it's time to call it a night?" Julie asked, stretching her arms and yawning dramatically.

Ben took her hand as they walked out to the parking lot. It had been a long day, but he felt all right. Tired, but content, allowing the shock of the deadly accident to recede slightly, he got behind the wheel of the rental and drove the six blocks to the apartment.

"Okay, I admit it. It's starting to look cool in here," Zac

said when they walked in.

Ben was pleased to see his son in better spirits.

"I'm going to sleep well tonight," Julie declared, dropping her purse on a chair.

Ben knew how she felt. The adrenaline of the move, the work, the anticipation—it all mixed with the grief of their recent loss, mingled with the relief of finally being here, of finally starting anew.

"It's a new beginning," Ben whispered. He glanced around at his family, at their new city. He could do this. They could do this.

It felt like things were finally looking up for them.

Chapter 11

They were eating breakfast when the sharp knock on the door startled them. Julie dropped her grapefruit spoon with a clatter, and Zac's Froot Loops tipped almost out of the bowl. Ben got up to see who was at their door at eight a.m. Through the peephole he spotted two uniformed state police officers. This couldn't be good. He opened the door only as wide as the safety chain.

"Yes?" His voice was wary.

"Mr. Pecos? Benson Pecos?"

"It's Doctor, and yes, that's me."

"We're here concerning a fatal traffic accident two days ago."

Ben glanced at the breakfast bar where Julie and Zac were staring wide-eyed. He tried to give them his most reassuring smile, but it was a faint one.

"Please, come in," he said, opening the door.

The two officers stepped inside. Ben wondered frantically if this was something the son of the victim should be hearing. "Julie," he said quietly, "maybe you and Zac should wait in the other room until I find out what this is about."

"Dad, no. I need to hear what they say."

Ben turned toward the officers. "We lost two family members in that accident, gentlemen. I'd appreciate your discretion."

"I understand, sir. There's been some new information in the case, apparently, and one of the detectives would like to speak with you at the station. We were sent to offer you a ride."

"Offer. So, it would be all right if I drive myself there?"

"Detective Herrera would like to talk with you this morning," said the older of the two.

"Please," added the other one.

"Do you know the nature of this new information?" Ben's mind was buzzing.

The senior officer shook his head. "You'll need to speak with Detective Herrera. Marcus Herrera." He handed over a card with the address and phone numbers of the state police station.

"I will drive myself and you may tell the detective that I will be there in about thirty minutes." Ben debated calling the number, asking for the detective, and trying to get information over the phone. But his past experiences with police in several jurisdictions had taught him that probably wouldn't work. They wanted to see your face.

He closed the door behind the retreating policemen.

"Ben, what on earth …?"

"I have no idea, but the only way to find out is for me to go over there and see what this detective wants."

"I should—" Julie looked at Zac. "*We* should come along."

"It's probably some routine notification, maybe a few questions …"

"And in that case, it won't take long." She was already stacking the breakfast dishes in the sink. "Afterward, we'll do as we'd planned this morning and go shopping for another vehicle. We can't always be in the same place all the time."

Ben met Zac's puzzled stare. "We'll get this figured out, son. Don't worry."

* * *

Exactly thirty minutes later Ben was seated across a desk from Marcus Herrera. Julie had protested slightly about being asked to wait in the lobby, but finally agreed that Ben should know what was going on before Zac heard it.

The man in front of Ben was in his mid-fifties, of average height with a solid build that spoke of regular gym workouts. Salt-and-pepper hair kept military short, clean-shaven. Prominent laugh lines contrasted with his serious expression. Ben took in the well-pressed slacks and the dress shirt under Herrera's dark jacket and noted the polished but comfortable shoes. His tone was businesslike, not antagonistic but not exactly friendly.

He led with the statement that the wreckage of Raven's car had been examined by the forensic team in Santa Fe. "The accident is now being considered a deliberate act."

Ben had expected there to be something surprising in an autopsy report, maybe some forbidden substance in Raven's system. This news came as a complete shock. He forced himself to focus on the man's voice.

"We believe it was intentional." The words were blunt, revealing something unthinkable.

A dull roar filled Ben's ears as he struggled to process. Nathan and Raven. Their car, tampered with? How and when could it have happened?

He must have said those words aloud because Herrera responded, "That's what we'd like to know. What can you tell us about that?"

The vivid blue sky outside the high windows felt at odds with the darkness that had suddenly descended inside. Ben felt himself stammering. "About the car? Nothing. I have no idea what happened."

Herrera's steady gaze shook Ben's confidence. He took a deep breath and forced himself to focus, to remain calm.

"Do you have any ideas about who might have wanted to harm Ms. Takanni?"

"Not offhand. We lived at opposite ends of the country, detective. She resided in Washington state; my wife and I were in Florida." He gave the briefest possible version of their connection, what they were all doing in New Mexico this week, and why they were on the road to Tewa Pueblo.

"You all spent the night before here in the city, at the Hotel Albuquerque." It wasn't a question.

Ben nodded, although he had no idea how the police knew this.

"Is there anything else you would like to add, Dr. Pecos?"

"I can't think of anything at the moment. I would

appreciate it if you could let me know of further developments—for the sake of our son."

Herrera stood, dismissing him. Ben walked out into the lobby, wondering how much of this he should share.

* * *

The car dealer's lot was the right place to distract Zac. While the teen rushed over to the section filled with sports cars, Ben and Julie ambled among the pickup trucks. He quickly shut down the salesperson who approached, and once the young woman walked away, he filled Julie in on what the detective had told him.

"Do you think it's connected to Raven's recent moodiness, some problem she had back in Washington?" Her voice was low, probing.

Ben hesitated. He had thought the same thing, but admitting it made it real. "I don't know," he replied. "It's possible. Herrera seemed to want to dig into her personal life and what was going on. I had to admit I knew nothing much about that."

Raven had been part of his life before he met Julie, before they knew about Zac. But, aside from the boy, nothing in her life today was connected to them. None of it made sense.

Julie's instincts were razor-sharp, honed by years of reporting. She could sniff out a story before anyone else saw it coming. But this wasn't just a story. It was their life. Their family.

"We need to wait for more information," Ben said, trying to sound more confident than he felt. "The police said they'd update us. Maybe they'll find something soon."

"Maybe," Julie allowed, though she didn't sound convinced.

Ben wanted to reassure her, but wasn't sure how. Zac was grieving, his wife was convinced there was some kind of story here, and Ben only wanted to get on with the new job he'd accepted.

"What do we do in the meantime?" Julie asked.

Ben didn't reply right away. He looked out toward Sandia Peak in the distance. They'd planned a new start here. Now it felt like they were being pulled back, tangled in something more vast than they could see.

"There's still a lot to handle. Herrera said there are autopsies, mandated because it's now considered a suspicious accident. Once that's done, Raven's body will have to be sent to her family. I'll need to deal with Nathan's." His throat tightened. Fleeting thoughts about what do to on that subject. "At some point I guess we'll need to get Zac's belongings from Bellingham—it may involve a trip there." He pulled Julie in close, hugging her to his chest. "We'll deal with it. Whatever it means."

Zac jogged over to them. "Dad, I found the coolest Corvette."

"I'm sure you did, son, but a truck comes first."

When Julie looked in his direction again, he met her gaze. He had to believe everything would work out all right.

Chapter 12

The new Chevy Silverado pickup truck sat in its parking slot in front of the apartment. Signing the paperwork, transferring money, trying to act upbeat in front of the saleslady who expected joyfulness from them. At last they'd escaped the dealership, returned Julie's rental car to the airport, and made a quick stop at a huge Walmart for a new TV before driving home. Tomorrow, with luck, they would find a vehicle for Julie, and the Pecos family would have wheels enough, for now. Eventually, once he learned the city layout better, and once they had some spare cash, Zac would likely get a starter car, too.

"Long day, huh," Julie said, walking up behind Ben and snaking her arms around his middle, resting her head against his back. "I think I want to find my sleep mask, the one I always put in the fridge before wearing. It relaxes me."

The apartment was unnervingly quiet, Zac having retreated to his room; the withdrawal added another layer of tension to an already strained atmosphere. "I'll check on him," Ben said, trying to hide his worry.

Julie turned toward a stack of boxes in one corner of the living room, studying the labels to remember where she'd packed the mask.

Zac was sprawled on his bed, headphones clamped over his ears. Ben could see the tension in his posture, the way his leg jiggled in a nervous tic.

"Hey, kiddo," Ben said.

Zac didn't respond right away. Ben touched his shoulder, and Zac looked up, startled.

"What?" Zac asked, pulling off the headphones. His tone was defensive, tense.

"Checking in," Ben said. "You've been quiet since we got home."

"Yeah, well. There's not a lot to say, is there?" Zac replied, his words sarcastic, but Ben heard the underlying fear. Ben felt a pang at the uncertainty in his son's eyes, a reflection of his own feelings.

"You want to talk?" Ben offered, hoping to coax Zac out of his shell.

Zac shook his head, his expression guarded. "Not really."

"It's okay to be scared." Ben was wary of the walls Zac was building around himself. "I am too."

"You?" Zac looked at him, surprised. Ben had always been the strong one, the stable center.

"Yeah, me," Ben confirmed. "A lot of things have changed in recent days. But we're going to get through this."

"How?" Zac's question was a plea for reassurance.

"By sticking together, learning what we can about the crash, hoping the police figure out what was behind it."

Zac nodded, though he didn't seem entirely convinced. It was a start, though, a crack in the shell.

Ben felt a rush of affection, of protectiveness. Time would help to heal this, but it wouldn't be a quick fix.

"Come out when you're ready," Ben said, giving Zac's shoulder a squeeze. "Julie said something about watching a movie on that new TV, making some popcorn."

"Okay," Zac said, quieter now, less defensive. He put the headphones back on, but Ben knew he was still listening, still present.

Ben left the room, wondering if he'd said all the right things. Julie was waiting, holding up a flat package wrapped in shiny gift paper. "Do you know what this is? I found it in the same box with things from the master bath at the other house. I've never seen it before."

Ben shook his head. He took the packet and examined it more closely, noticing the careful way it was wrapped in bright gift paper. It was about six inches square, maybe an inch tall.

"I suppose one of the old neighbors might have tucked it in, a going-away present."

"There's no tag, no card. A neighbor would have handed it to us directly. Do you think Raven might have—?" Julie's voice trailed off, leaving the question hanging.

He weighed it in his hand. It was light, deceptively so.

"She didn't have access to the boxes inside that van," Ben said. "I'm sure of it."

Julie was silent, processing. Ben felt her puzzlement, mingling with his own.

"Maybe it got mixed up with our things," she suggested, but her voice lacked conviction.

"Mixed up, from where?" Ben countered, his thoughts spiraling.

"Maybe Zac knows. He helped unload and unpack a bunch of it. Maybe he slipped it in there as a gift."

He looked toward Zac's room. The kid was not adept at keeping secrets. Every birthday and Christmas had him itching to tell everyone what their presents were.

"We should open it," Julie suggested.

"I'll check with Zac first," he said, "in case it's his." He moved into Zac's room, getting his son's attention and waving the package. "Is this something of yours?"

Zac took a moment to focus his attention away from the music in his earbuds, but his blank look told Ben right away that his son knew nothing about it.

"Okay, never mind." Ben walked back into the living room.

They both looked at the package, its gaudy wrapping. "Are you ready?" he asked Julie.

"Oh, for Pete's sake, open it!" she said with a laugh. "We'll never know who gave it to us if we don't look inside." She reached out and ripped the paper.

Inside was a smaller package, wrapped in plain paper. The double wrapping and lack of ornamentation was weird. Ben felt Julie's eyes on him, waiting, as he lifted the second package from the box. Ben hesitated, then tore the paper in one rip.

Inside that, a sealed, plain brown envelope. Ben turned it over, half expecting to see a name or greeting. But it was blank, unmarked. He looked at Julie, his confusion matching hers.

Ben ripped the seal. There was no note, no explanation. Only a photo, glossy and new, in a cheap metal frame. It was Zac, unmistakably. A picture of him from last spring break, when they'd taken a trip to the Everglades. He was smiling, unaware. Ben remembered the day. He and Nathan could have easily been in the photo too. The familiarity of it was like a punch to the gut.

Julie's hand flew to her mouth. "Oh my God, Ben. Who could've taken this? And worse … how did it get into our household boxes?"

Ben stared at the image, his thoughts tangled. This felt personal.

And more frightening, could it somehow be related to what happened to Raven and Nathan? The crash, the package—maybe connected?

The idea settled in, chilling and urgent. "Should we inform Detective Herrera about this?"

Julie nibbled at her lower lip. "I don't think so, not yet. We don't *know* that it's connected to Raven in any way. She wasn't with you on that vacation trip. We should find out if there's a connection before involving the police."

"How? We don't even know where to start."

"We could call Raven's family," Julie said with sudden certainty. "See what they know."

The thought of involving the Takanni clan didn't sound appealing, but it might be the only way. Raven might have confided things to her brother that she didn't want anyone else to know. He needed to make a condolence call to them anyway, should have done so already.

"Okay," Ben agreed, the word sounding heavy. He looked at the photo one last time. "I'll call E.J."

Chapter 13

Raven's brother, E.J. Takanni, had once been Ben's roommate and friend, back in college. Needless to say, the relationship took a turn for the cooler when E.J. learned Ben had dated his sister and fathered a child with her. It didn't matter that Ben knew nothing about Zac's existence until the boy was ten. Eventually, a workable—if not exactly cordial—relationship evolved with the other Takannis, a family whose history was complex and messy.

Ben dialed E.J.'s number, but as soon as he identified himself on the phone, E.J.'s voice went cold.

"You. I suppose you're happy now." So much for his accepting Ben's condolences.

"E.J.! Of course not. We're all devastated over what happened."

"More devastated than when you screamed at her

about keeping Zac for the holidays? Call me skeptical."

So, Raven had spoken with her brother after their disagreement over the boys' visitation. He wanted to ask what was said, but knew better. This wasn't about getting a blow-by-blow account of Raven's side of things. He took a deep breath and brought up the subject of the mysterious photo found among their things.

"Pah. No idea. What you and that wife of yours do with your own possessions is no business of mine."

Julie bristled. Probably a mistake to put the call on speaker. Ben gave her a steady look and rubbed the back of her hand.

"I want my sister back, here in Alaska, to receive a proper burial," E.J. was saying. "And that cop wouldn't tell me when that's going to happen."

Cop? Apparently E.J. had spoken to Herrera. Julie was making frantic motions to wind up the phone call, mouthing *don't say anything.*

"We don't know, either. Sorry," Ben said. "I'll let you go now." He ended the call without waiting for a response.

"What the hell?" Julie muttered.

This couldn't be good.

The next morning, when the same two state police officers arrived at their door during breakfast, it was not a friendly request. They wanted Ben to ride to the station with them. At least they skipped the handcuffs.

* * *

Julie's phone kept buzzing like a demented bee trapped in a glass jar. Her Florida story had hit the news cycle, including social media; congratulatory texts and emails were pouring in from all over the country. Yet, pacing the lobby of the NMSP station, all the joy evaporated. She could only see the tangled web around Ben's situation.

Unanswered questions about the hotel confrontation between Ben and Raven twisted her gut. All she had was Ben's version, that it was nothing substantial, and yet she knew the bitterness that existed in the Takanni family. Raven's version of the events recounted to her brother, a lawyer, and passed along to the police, was surely less benign.

Julie rubbed her temples as the pressure mounted. Her professional life had taken off like a rocket, but her personal life felt like it was in freefall. She should be putting out feelers for a new job, hoping to be grabbed up while her star was on the rise. Instead, she sank into a chair, feeling helpless.

She imagined what was happening now—the police grilling Ben according to their version of the evidence. The tampering with Raven's car, an argument with her ex, his being out in the parking lot late in the evening—it wouldn't paint a pretty picture.

He'd denied threatening her, but even Julie had been surprised at the intensity of his, and Raven's, feelings on the subject. If *she'd* been surprised, what did that mean for how it looked to strangers? Could she blame the police for their conclusions?

The sound of the station's phones ringing, feet shuffling on the hard floor, and low voices filled the lobby. She ran a hand through her curls, glancing again at her phone's insistent notifications. Each new alert about her big story felt like an anomaly. The contrast couldn't be starker: professional triumph on one hand, personal devastation on the other.

The memory of the look on Ben's face when they'd led him out to the waiting cruiser. His voice, calmly telling her to wait at the apartment. She felt the urgency to *do* something—anything—so she had followed. Now, sitting in the waiting room, she was in limbo until she heard what the detectives had to say.

The desk officer glanced at her with something like pity, and her pulse quickened. Did he know something? Had Ben asked him to keep an eye on her—did he even know she was here? She stood abruptly, itching to move, if only to pace the floor.

In her work, she had usually been the one in control, unraveling other people's stories and presenting them on her terms. Now she was in the middle of a personal narrative, and it terrified her. What did this mean for them, for their family? What would happen to Zac if Ben was taken away? She fought the creeping sensation of panic as she replayed everything in her mind, trying to connect the dots.

Zac's voice echoed in her head from when she'd gathered her purse and keys and told him to stay inside the apartment. "They're not going to arrest Dad, are they?" She'd said all the reassuring things, but now she wondered.

The whir of the ceiling fan and the hum of traffic from the street filled her ears as she sank back into the chair, trying to keep herself from unraveling.

The door opened, and a lean figure strode into the lobby. His dark suit held sharp, precise lines, and his hair was salted with gray. "Mrs. Pecos?" he asked, scanning a clipboard without looking up. "Detective Herrera. Do you have a moment?" His voice was as clipped and efficient as his appearance.

"Of course," Julie said, trying to match his detachment. Her legs felt like rubber. He motioned for her to follow, and the knot in her chest pressed heavier with each step. She glanced back at the desk officer, who was suddenly busy with something else.

Herrera led her down a long hallway to an interrogation room. The walls were institutional gray, bare except for a whiteboard, and a table with a folder placed squarely at its center. "Your husband thought you might have some insights," he said, gesturing for her to sit. The detective seemed too composed, the kind of man who measured everything twice. She thought of her early reporting days, dealing with men like this. Not easy, but not impossible either.

"Where is Ben now?" She imagined a cell and a mug shot. Or maybe an interrogation room identical to this one.

Herrera remained standing, looming slightly over the table. "This is a serious matter. We've had a witness come forward." He let the words hang, then opened the folder, flipping through the pages. "What can you tell me about an argument that took place between your husband and Ms. Takanni?"

Julie's pulse quickened. Although she'd known this was coming, she tried to swallow her panic, keeping her face a neutral canvas, as she had learned when interviewing her own tricky subjects. "I don't know anything. I wasn't present."

He wasn't going to accept that as an answer. "But what about the general mood? You were all together at dinner, conversed in the hotel lobby."

"There was some tension that night. Family dynamics." She made herself meet his eyes. "People do say things they regret."

"Not usually the night before someone winds up dead," Herrera replied, without skipping a beat. "And then there's the matter of Dr. Pecos's unaccounted time. How long was he away from your room when he said he went down to the parking lot?"

"I don't know. I was asleep when he left the room. Based on when he returned, it had to be less than an hour. Maybe thirty minutes."

Julie flinched at her own words. She should have kept the timeframe precise, but she simply didn't remember looking at the clock.

"*Maybe* an hour. *Maybe* thirty minutes? That's a pretty wide range, considering it was a five-minute walk to and from your room."

Julie couldn't shake the sense that this was a performance, designed to push her buttons.

"Does Ben need a lawyer?" she asked, careful not to let the fear show in her voice.

"Depends on whether he can explain some of these questions."

She leaned forward, letting silence stretch out. She'd learned in her own investigations that silence could make people say more than they intended. But Herrera was a pro; he simply waited her out.

She took a breath and shifted tactics, trying to seem cooperative. "When the police knocked on our door, I assumed it was to give us some updated news. Instead, it seems you're spending a lot of time building a case on pure speculation." Her words came out sharper than she'd intended.

Herrera arched an eyebrow. "Your husband didn't seem surprised when we showed up."

His words stung. "He's a psychologist, Detective. He's

trained to hold it together even when he's shaken to the core. But I suppose you have him all figured out already, don't you?"

Julie realized she was coming across too defensive, too emotional. It wasn't how she wanted to play this. She forced herself to slow down. "If you've got witnesses, we'd like to see their statements. And as for unaccounted time, I'm sure Ben explained where he was. Are you charging him with something?"

"Not yet, Mrs. Pecos. Not yet." He glanced at his watch, then back to her, a hint of condescension in the way he cocked his head. She wondered if he was playing a game to see who would crack first. Maybe she was falling right into it.

"May I see Ben now?" she asked, her voice steadier than she expected.

"Soon," Herrera said, gathering the papers back into the folder with deliberate care. "We'll have more questions, I'm sure. The more you can remember, the better for everyone."

Julie nodded, her strength returning as the initial shock wore off. Her resolve stiffened with every step as she left the room. Ben needed her to be strong, to help him untangle this mess. The police's suspicions felt both ridiculous and terrifying, but she knew she had to hold it together, to be strong and focus on Ben and the facts no matter how impossible the situation felt. Herrera didn't know it, but Julie had resources of her own and was ready to use them.

She pushed her way outside, cutting across the parking lot to where Ben stood next to the new pickup. He hurried toward her, noting the spark in her eyes. "I was starting to worry," he said, unable to mask his relief at seeing her. "Herrera didn't push too hard?"

"Not yet. Not as hard as we have to push. Ben, I think we need to go on the offensive here." She climbed into the passenger seat, already thinking ten steps ahead, as if the detective's conversation had given her more than it took away. "I need to talk to Monica, an old friend over at the *Journal*. And some of my other old contacts. If we're going to do this, we have to act now."

He gave her an admiring look as he started the truck. "You're sure journalists can help?"

"I'm sure they can't hurt." She fastened her seatbelt, pulled out her phone, and dialed. "Monica! It's Julie. Do you have a minute?" Her fingers tapped impatiently against the door handle. "Look, I need a huge favor. Can you dig into your police scanner archives from three days ago?"

* * *

Ben waited for traffic to clear and pulled into the far left-hand lane on Menaul, ready to make the left turn onto Carlisle, as she continued. He had to admit Julie gave just enough detail to get her former colleague's attention, not enough to hint that the matter was extremely personal for them. It was brilliant and a little scary to watch her work like this, like a relentless force of nature.

Julie's voice was sharp, authoritative, cutting through any questions on the other end. "No, nothing from the reporters. Not yet. I'd like the raw audio if you can get it." A pause, then more softly, "Thanks, Monica. I owe you big time."

She hung up and turned to Ben. "We need to follow

everything. What Herrera said about witnesses. About unaccounted time. If someone saw something, we need to know what that was."

Her conviction was infectious, and Ben found himself drawn into her urgency despite the twist in his stomach. "You think the police missed something? Or they want it to look like I'm guilty?"

She met his eyes, unflinching. "They've already made up their minds, Ben. It's up to us to change them."

Her words sent both dread and encouragement through him. She was diving headfirst into the chaos for his sake, and all he could do was hang on and hope.

She made two more calls, pressing her contacts to dig deeper and faster. It was like watching her in the newsroom, a whirlwind of efficiency and passion, but now the stakes were *so* personal. Her voice was professional, but Ben heard the strain beneath it.

Ben admired her skill, how she handled each person differently, knowing exactly which buttons to press. But beneath that admiration was a gnawing worry: *the police have made up their minds*. He felt the desperation, the need to find answers before they came for him with a warrant for his arrest.

"I don't know what we're looking for," she admitted to Ben when there was a rare moment of silence. "Just that we're looking."

"And until we find it?" he asked.

She took his hand, her grip fierce. "Until we find it, I won't stop."

Ben felt a wave of gratitude and guilt. She was putting everything on the line for him. He felt absolutely blessed by how fiercely she loved him.

He was making the turn from San Mateo to Academy when Julie's phone rang, jolting them both from their thoughts. She grabbed it, holding the phone to her ear. The call was brief, and her expression unreadable.

"Anything new?" he asked, once she'd ended the call.

"Not much. We're trying to get a look at the hotel's security camera footage."

He nodded, trying to share her hope, trying to imagine how that parking lot encounter would appear to the unemotional camera lens.

When they got back to the apartment, Julie didn't pause before diving in again. Booting up her laptop, she pored over news articles and scanned online forums, searching for any coverage of the accident that might give them a lead. Ben felt like a ghost as he paced the living room, unable to join her frantic energy.

"I don't suppose you'd like to take a break and go look at some cars?" he suggested, thinking they could get some relief from the intensity of the muddy combination of grieving, settling in after the cross-country move, and now potentially being a murder suspect. But Julie barely heard him. She shook her head, her eyes never leaving her computer screen.

"Okay then, I think I'll see if Zac wants to go out for a burger or something."

Again, only a tiny nod. Julie seemed more focused than ever, but Ben could sense her frustration simmering beneath the surface.

Chapter 14

Julie felt like pulling her hair out. She was too close to the story to be objective, and she knew it. What if all her efforts led nowhere? But she had to keep trying.

Her friend, Monica, at the *Journal* had quickly come up with recordings of the police scanner radio band for the morning of the accident. The 10-codes and police-speak revealed only what Julie already knew—there'd been a highway accident, mile marker numbers given, there were fatalities. Police, ambulances, and a helicopter were dispatched.

After that, the airwaves went silent, probably to keep nosy reporters away. Julie knew the results of those calls, but she thanked Monica profusely and said now that she was back in town, they should do lunch. They probably wouldn't. It wasn't that close of a friendship. Still, it was always smart to keep contacts active in this business.

David Griego, a guy she remembered from one of the local TV networks, answered her call on the first ring. They'd collaborated on a story, years earlier, and now he wanted to meet her for coffee. For one second, she considered it. A business meeting was deductible, after all. But then she remembered—she had no vehicle. She needed to remedy that soon; this city was too sprawled out, Uber would get expensive, and public transportation wasn't much of an option.

"Or a drink this evening?" he said, breaking into her thoughts.

"Afraid anything resembling a date is out. I'm married now, David." At his disappointed reaction, she didn't have the heart to tell him she was looking for a defense for her husband.

She brought up the accident, saying only that she'd been on the road at the same time and saw all the fuss. Her hopes for some gossipy insider news were dashed, though.

He recalled the event and only commented that it was one of many. "The highways of New Mexico are known for being bloody, a deadly combination of wide-open spaces, high speeds, and frequent alcohol use." It was an insensitive thing to say, even though it was true.

When the call ended, she got up for a glass of water and went back to stare at her computer screen. Okay, there had to be other avenues. Since Raven knew no one in town, there simply weren't viable local suspects. But something in her past must be related. Someone had come to the point of tampering with her car, knowing the result would be serious. And, dammit, that person was not Julie's gentle, caring husband.

She sat down again and did the most logical thing—

Googled Raven's name. Several results sprang to the top of the list, all connected to the Iditarod dogsled race and the Takanni family's prominence in that sport. It was, for the most part, a friendly rivalry among people who knew each other, but the competition could be fierce. The purse for this year's race was over half a million dollars, plus gold nuggets and other prizes. That would have been huge money for a woman who complained bitterly if Ben's support check didn't show up at the minute it was due.

Julie jotted a few notes and names. She went to the race's history page to find out the winners in recent years. Raven was there in the past, five years in a row, but she hadn't placed since she moved to Washington full-time. That made sense—she didn't have the time to practice or work with her dogs if she wasn't in Alaska as much of the year.

Three names stood out in the list of recent winners, all from a family named Hill. That was a common enough name to have residents anywhere, and she knew a search of Hills in New Mexico would be useless. Plus, why would the Hills come after Raven now? She hadn't been a serious threat to their family dynasty in a while.

Or had she?

Another thing Julie remembered about Raven—she tended to be a troublemaker. An activist on numerous subjects, from gas pipelines to animal rights, all of which were worthy. But sometimes a person's loud mouth and brash ways got them in trouble, even when their outspokenness was for the best of causes. Julie chided herself for thinking of Raven as loud and brash, even though it was true some of the time.

Before she had the chance to search some of the other

topics Raven had been associated with, she heard the sound of a key in the lock.

"We brought you lunch from Lotaburger," Ben said, holding up the white bag with the red and blue logo she remembered so well. "An Itsa with cheese and green chile."

"My heroes. I hadn't even realized it, but I'm starving." She closed her laptop and set it atop her pile of notes, indulging in a quick fantasy of having a real home office once they got settled.

Zac switched on the new TV but kept the volume reasonably low. Ben sipped the remainder of his gigantic soft drink while Julie began to devour her burger.

"I didn't mean to blow off your suggestion about shopping for another car earlier," she said between mouthfuls. "You're right. We need two. After next week, when you get started with IHS, it sounds like you'll be on the road a lot. Zac and I will need a way to get around."

Ben glanced toward his son. "We need to get him enrolled in school. The boarding school he attended in Bellingham had an autumn break, which they were using for the trip here, but Albuquerque schools don't have that. I don't want him falling behind."

She nodded agreement. "Shall we begin the car shopping online or visit a dealership?"

A quick search showed a dozen dealerships within a ten-minute range of their apartment. "Looks like you can take your pick, from a Porsche to a VW," Ben said, as Julie wadded up the wrappers from her lunch and tossed them in the wastebasket.

"I'd love to say I'm a Porsche kind of girl, but if I'm to get a job in journalism I need to stay more low-key than that. Plus, I'd love to take a look at the new hybrids."

"Not to mention, we'd better hang on to some of that insurance money for furnishing that house we're now apparently buying."

Was Ben experiencing sticker shock over the money they'd spent recently? Probably. Julie certainly was. "How about that CarMax place along the interstate? A used one will suit me fine."

No one said it, but the specter of having to hire a defense attorney was also out there on the horizon.

* * *

The pungent scent of chrysanthemums filtered across the car lot from the beautifully planted landscaping. They'd signed papers for a nice, three-year-old Toyota hybrid, and Julie had the keys in her hand. Ben climbed in his truck and she led the way back toward the apartment, windows down and the breeze in her face.

The breath of fresh air jolted her back to what she needed to do. Ben was innocent. That much was certain, and there had to be a way to prove it before the authorities came to arrest him. As a family, they'd managed to get the practicalities of their move taken care of in a few days' time. Now she needed to get serious in her search for whoever had actually set up Raven Takanni to die.

Would it be someone from Raven's activist past or something else? Could it be somehow related to her recent moodiness? Julie didn't know, but she had to start somewhere. She reminded herself any lead was a good lead, and a sharp investigative reporter never knew which of them would pay off.

Zac was in the kitchen, facing into the refrigerator,

when they walked in.

"I was thinking we could bake those two frozen pizzas for dinner tonight," Julie said.

She received a grunt in return. Ben was no more successful when he asked if Zac wanted to see the new car. The teen stomped into his room and closed the door, a little too hard.

"Okay … what was that?"

Ben let out a long breath. "Let's give him a few minutes and then I'll talk to him."

"You look pooped, Ben. Why don't you grab a nap?" She couldn't remember a time in their married life when Ben had needed an afternoon nap. But there'd never been a time in their lives together when there was so much at stake. Plus, she could use the uninterrupted time for some more online research.

As soon as he disappeared into their bedroom, she opened her laptop and looked at the tabs she'd kept open. The subject of the Iditarod had not shown her an immediate answer, but she left the search results there and clicked to open a new tab. This time she went to social media to see if Raven hung out there at all. She found profiles on Facebook, Instagram, and TikTok.

The first two platforms contained personal data and profile photos of Raven with Zac and Nathan. On TikTok, it seemed she mainly concentrated on her tattoo business. After watching a couple of videos of Raven applying ink to customers, Julie began to scroll faster. This wasn't what she was interested in, fascinating as it was to recall the process from when Raven had done the beautiful feather tat on Julie's shoulder.

Back to Facebook, where people tended to be more

wordy and often engaged with others, often in a nice way, sometimes not. She found posts where Raven announced her arrival in Albuquerque with a snide remark: "Nothing green to be seen here, can't wait to turn around for home in a week!"

Julie caught herself looking out the window where she saw plenty of green. But true, desert green didn't compare to the Pacific Northwest.

Raven's next-earlier posts were taken along the road trip, photos of the giant donut the boys had mentioned, and a caption: "Glad to get away from the tension in Seattle."

Hmm … what tension was that? Julie scrolled back on the timeline to find out.

A post Raven wrote two weeks before the trip caught her attention: "WTF! Whoever tore up my shop had better come forward with a check to pay for the damages. I've called the cops. They have your fingerprints all over the place."

More than a hundred comments followed, everything from supportive emojis and 'Oh-no!' to several that devolved into arguments over the quality of Raven's shop and how much better the new one on the other side of town was.

Had Raven mentioned vandalism at her tattoo shop during their dinner in Old Town? Or a competitor who appeared to be stealing her customers? Julie didn't think so. But it could definitely account for the woman's grumpy demeanor and constant scrolling on her phone.

Raven's Facebook responses to the ugly comments had begun to grow downright nasty. Julie was only partway through the lengthy exchanges when Zac's bedroom door opened. She hastily closed her laptop.

She mustered her brightest smile. "Hey there. I was thinking about some dinner. You hungry?"

He shrugged with that non-caring look teens have perfected. But when the door to the other bedroom opened and Ben stepped out, the boy's demeanor softened.

"Did somebody say pizza?" Ben held up a fist to exchange one of those complicated bump-slap-reverse moves with his son.

Julie cleared her notes and computer off the table while they baked the frozen pizzas. Ben loved thin crust and a white cream sauce, while she and Zac preferred the thick one with marinara sauce and tons of pepperoni, and she was glad she'd purchased one of each. They didn't come close to what they'd enjoyed at Dion's a couple nights ago, but they couldn't afford to eat out for every meal.

Over dinner, the subject turned to school. Ben had checked on the districts for both their current neighborhood and the one where the new house was located. He brought up his findings—the present neighborhood had the newer school, but they wouldn't be living in the apartment much longer and it was a fairly long haul across the city for a daily commute.

While he and Julie discussed the merits of the two choices, Zac remained largely unengaged. When Ben asked his opinion directly, he ignored the question.

"Okay, we can plan a visit to each of them and see what you think," Ben said, knowing when to let a subject rest.

When Julie suggested a movie, Zac slumped off to his room again. At least this time he closed the door more gently.

"What's with all this?" she asked Ben as the two of them cleared the dishes and neatened up the kitchen.

"In my professional opinion? A lot of it is grief, and a lot of it is normal teenage sullenness. They're both things he'll get past, eventually, but for us it could be a long haul."

Julie sighed. "Okay, it is what it is." Then she proceeded to fill him in on her online research. "Did Raven say anything to you about a threat to her business? Maybe this competitor was behind the vandalism to her shop, and maybe they even threatened her."

Ben thought for a long moment. "I don't think so. I got the idea something was going on, but she didn't discuss her business. You know Raven. She had a history of rabble-rousing. Activism that spilled into fanaticism, as some might call it. Two years ago, she threatened to put a stop to the construction of a gas line when it exploded and killed a handful of bystanders. She believed the explosion was deliberate and she was supposed to be one of the victims, and then she stepped right up and announced she would testify against the company in court."

Those types of actions didn't win a girl a lot of friends, Julie thought.

"There were lawsuits involved and Raven, in true form, had managed to make some truly dangerous enemies. Are you thinking one of them might even have the stomach to arrange a fatal accident in the hope of scaring her off?"

"I don't know, Ben. I just don't know."

"Be careful, sweetheart. You don't know who you're dealing with."

He was right about that—she didn't know. But she had to find out. They had to steer the police toward somebody else.

Chapter 15

His coffee was cold again. Paperwork from the Indian Health Service waited to be addressed, information Sandy Black wanted him to study before he reported for work. Ben's swirling thoughts had disrupted his sleep until he finally got up at four a.m. Thinking the paperwork would provide a distraction and a coffee would clear his head, he found that his concerns for Zac, his grief over Nathan, and the thundercloud of suspicion that hung over him … it all looped without resolution.

Daylight began to show at the windows. He should trade his pajama pants for real ones. But he sat unmoving at the kitchen table so Julie could sleep a while longer. His mind traveled to the previous day, picturing Zac's hardening expression during their visits to two high school campuses. Angry and resistant, his son had trudged through hallways, shoulders stiff with words he refused to say to the counselors they met with.

The transformation had been swift and fierce since Raven's death, turning a bright and curious boy into someone unfamiliar, someone who met every attempt with anger or apathy. It was a grief Ben could deal with in a client, a stranger, but with his own son it felt like a knot tightening by the day, not to mention a professional slap in the face.

He sighed and looked again at the cold coffee. As if mirroring his own mood, it had become lifeless and unappealing, a metaphor for his efforts to reach Zac. The outing yesterday—the campus visits followed by lunch in a park, had been Ben's attempt to create a space for his son to talk, to open up about Raven and everything that had been left unsaid. Instead, they had eaten in silence, the warm sun casting dappled shadows on the grass.

Ben heard a door open and heavy footsteps approaching. He steeled himself as Zac came into the room, his hair unkempt and face set in a now-familiar scowl. The teenager moved with deliberate avoidance, heading straight for the fridge and yanking the door open. Zac kept his back turned, his silence saying more than words would. Ben had a brief memory of Raven and the way she reacted to stress when he'd first known her.

"Hey, Zac," Ben tried, keeping his voice neutral and gentle. "You have plans today?"

Zac paused without turning around. "Maybe," he muttered, rooting through the shelves as if the contents were responsible for his discontent.

Ben tamped down his impatience. He knew these were Raven's habits emerging—this silent fuming, the refusal to engage—but knowing didn't make it any easier. "I thought maybe we could hang out a bit," Ben ventured. "Maybe grab some lunch, see a movie?"

Zac turned enough for Ben to catch the edge of his glare. "I'm in the middle of a game." He held up his iPad and then walked out before Ben could respond.

Ben sat there, the fridge door banging shut, leaving a vibrating tension in the air. He was torn, professional instincts at war with paternal love. Every book and training session told him to give Zac space, to let him come to terms with Raven's death in his own time. But Ben worried that his son was slipping away, the breach widening with every curt reply.

He stared at the cup in front of him, wanting to shatter its cool detachment. Instead, he reached for it, trying to find some small comfort in its familiar weight, when his phone rang sharply beside him.

The caller ID made him pause: Rynah Takanni, sister to Raven's late mother, Ahnah. E.J. had insisted that Ben should have her number as a Takanni family contact. He barely remembered her, as she'd moved to Wasilla right after Ben's assignment in Moose Flats. Rynah was an attorney, same as E.J., and his impression during their one meeting was that she and Ahnah could have been twins. Ben's stomach tightened.

He picked up the phone, trying to steady his voice, unsure whether he felt relief or dread. "Hello, Rynah."

There was a slight pause on the line, the silence heavy. When Rynah spoke, her voice was as Ben remembered—direct and unyielding, this time colored by an understandable kind of sorrow. "Benson. I want my niece returned. Why has this taken so long?"

Ben had anticipated the question, but her abruptness caught him off guard. He took a deep breath, reminded himself to respect Rynah's position as the current family matriarch, to tread carefully around her grief. "The medical investigator is taking longer than expected. I've called, but they haven't released the report yet. As soon as I know something, I promise—"

"Raven needs to be home," Rynah interrupted. "She has been gone too long. We will come to New Mexico."

Ben knew she would insist, had sensed from the conversations with E.J. that the family's patience was wearing thin. "I understand," he said, choosing his words carefully. "But I want to make sure everything is in order before you make the trip. I don't want you to come all this way and still be waiting."

"We will be there," Rynah repeated. "E.J. and I … we will come." Her voice faltered for a moment, a crack in her otherwise unyielding manner.

Ben felt for her, he truly did. "I'll keep you updated, Rynah. I want this to be right for everyone. I know how important this is."

There was a pause, then: "It is."

As Ben hung up the phone, he realized Zac had been standing in the alcove by his bedroom, out of sight but within earshot. When he stepped forward, his face was a storm of emotions—anger, confusion, an edge of something vulnerable that he quickly buried beneath a hard glare. Zac turned and left the apartment, slamming the door so hard the windows rattled. Ben winced but let him go.

He looked at the silent phone, wondering how he could meet the demands of Raven's family, Zac's needs, and his own sense of failure—failure to keep Raven and Nathan safe. The thought was a vivid reminder that Raven was not the only one who died. Zac's grief was not only for his mother, but for his adopted brother and best friend.

And Ben knew—adopted or not, Nathan was Diné. He belonged on the land of the Navajo Nation, with his tribe. Just as Ben would ultimately want to have his earthly remains at Tewa, he owed it to this boy to take him home.

* * *

Ben set his phone aside, worn out from a series of fruitless calls—to the medical investigator's office, to the county morgue, and finally to the one person who might remember him at the Navajo Tribal offices. Zac had returned a few minutes earlier, having walked down the street to the convenience store; two candy bars were the evidence. Ben rose, already weary from lack of sleep and a day that had not accomplished much, and headed down the hallway. He knocked on Zac's door tentatively, wishing Julie were there to add a soft touch but she'd left hours earlier on some secret mission.

No response. An impasse, like so many lately. Ben hesitated, then slowly opened the door, knowing Zac's silence was a command to leave him alone. He went in anyway, found his son hunched over his iPad, sitting on his bed. Ben sat at the far edge, fighting the sense of exclusion, of being an intruder in his own son's life.

Zac sat with his back turned, didn't acknowledge Ben's presence.

He cleared his throat gently, trying to break through the wall of silence. "Zac," Ben began, keeping his voice soft. "I know you're hurting. This isn't easy for any of us."

Zac's shoulders tensed, but he didn't respond. Ben waited, giving him space to react. When nothing came, he continued, aware of the precariousness of the moment. "Raven raised you alone for a long time. I know I can't replace her. I wouldn't try. But I'm here for you, whenever you're ready."

The teenager shifted slightly, his body language caught between anger and vulnerability. It was as if he was struggling to find the words but refused to give them a voice. The silence stretched on.

Ben watched him. He wanted to pull Zac into an embrace, to take away the hurt, but his instincts told him it wasn't time yet. So, he sat there, patient but aching, waiting for a sign, any sign, that his son would let him back in.

Nothing came.

He let out a breath he didn't know he'd been holding. "I'm going to give you some time," Ben said, rising slowly, reluctant to leave but knowing Zac needed the space. "I'll be here when you're ready to talk."

Zac remained with his head bowed over the screen in his lap, lost in thoughts that Ben could only imagine. He left the room quietly, closing the door with a softness that belied his inner torment. The rooms in the apartment felt emptier than usual, and he walked through them, caught between sorrow for his son and frustration with himself. He should have known what to say, but nothing seemed right.

Back at the dining table, he sank into a chair and let his thoughts unfurl. Parenting was a challenge under the best of circumstances, but going from barely part-time at this to doing it in the wake of tragedy felt insurmountable.

His training, his professional instincts—they all seemed inadequate to the task. Ben knew he had to be the constant in the chaos, the steady presence that Zac could turn to when he was ready.

The prospect of Raven's family arriving added another layer to the already complicated emotions. Ben could only imagine the strain it would put on Zac, having E.J. and Rynah here with their own grief and expectations. Then again, it might be what Zac needed, a connection to his mother's world that Ben could never fully provide.

Ben let out a weary sigh and reached for the cold cup of coffee, carrying it to the microwave, the simple act grounding him as he began to strategize how to handle the upcoming visit. He would need to balance sensitivity with pragmatism, ensuring that Rynah and E.J. were respected while protecting Zac's fragile state. It felt like a daunting task.

He set the cup back on the table, reaching for the documents pertaining to his new job. And then his phone rang. He startled at the vibrating sound, then looked at the name on the screen.

Office of the Medical Investigator.

Chapter 16

That evening he laid it out for Julie and Zac, his decision to follow the vehicle with Nathan's body and take him home to the Navajo reservation. The last time they'd been there, Zac was an inquisitive eleven-year-old, Nathan the older and street-wiser of them. The boys had bonded immediately. Now he was making plans to bury one. Ben had a hard time holding it together as he delivered the news that he would go the following morning.

"Zac, I'd love for you to come with me. Saying goodbye to your brother, seeing his final resting place … it's difficult, but it's also an important way to gain closure."

Zac nodded, his face a solemn mask.

"Do you want me to come along?" Julie asked.

"Your choice." Ben wasn't sure how to answer.

"I think it will be a day for the two of you to spend

together," she said, taking both of their hands and squeezing. "You need this time."

* * *

Ben stepped from his pickup truck onto the red earth of the Navajo Nation, a few miles south of Shiprock. The barren landscape echoed the emptiness he felt, so he turned toward the cluster of buildings that made up this remote community, Nathan's home. He took a moment to breathe and gather his thoughts. He recognized the schoolhouse, and it seemed that quite a few of the temporary trailer homes brought in for an emergency medical facility during the covid pandemic had now become permanent. What he didn't realize was that the community had established a cemetery, only last year.

A tall figure approached, and Ben recognized him as Clarence Benally, father of the police chief Ben had worked so closely with the last time he was here. The elder greeted him. "Yá'át'ééh, Benson."

"Ahéhee'," he replied, using one of the few Diné words he'd picked up during his time here. "We spoke last night. Thank you for your help."

Clarence had completely understood Ben's request; since Nathan had been born here and lived on the rez for his first thirteen years, it was only right that this be his final resting place, even though the teen had no living relatives since the pandemic.

Clarence nodded, his face solemn as he inquired how the rest of the family was coping. Ben glanced toward Zac; he didn't have much of an answer for that. They began walking, the elder reminding them of the rites practiced by Diné people. Ben knew that it was important not to entice the dead to return among the living, so there were to be no outward signs of grief or emotion, no familiar places, such as a family home, that the spirit might want to inhabit.

"I suggest this as the most appropriate place for young Nathan," Clarence told him as they walked past the school, across an open field and into a small plot of land with a low wall built of stacked rocks. The vehicle from the medical investigator's office—something arranged by Sandy Black, thankfully—had pulled up to the opening in the rock wall.

"The tribal council has recently set regulations to blend traditional customs with modern practices. The grounds are tended minimally, to keep the natural setting intact," Clarence told him. "Headstones or markers are allowed, even though that is a much more modern custom."

Ben saw at once that the new cemetery held a few dozen graves, most likely a residual of the pandemic's ravages among the people here.

He appreciated the landscape's austere beauty. The juniper and low piñon trees seemed to lean with the wind, stubborn and enduring. It reminded him of how Nathan had approached life, combining stubborn youthful energy with surprising maturity. Now, Ben was faced with the responsibility of bringing Nathan's spirit back to the land, ensuring that this part of his journey was dignified and respectful.

Zac trailed behind, his tall, youthful figure nearly a mirror of his dad. He'd rarely spoken during the three-and-a-half-hour drive. Ben had left him to his own thoughts and connections to Nathan.

Clarence paused to point toward an open grave beneath a solitary juniper. "There, we have prepared the way. Whenever you are ready." A few people walked over to join them; Ben recognized Trini Lovato, the invaluable assistant he'd worked with, and one of the other women.

He felt a tug of emotion that nearly overwhelmed him. A mixture of gratitude and loss swept through him. Memories of Nathan, as his face had glowed when they made s'mores during their camping trip together, the excitement as the young lad had insisted on taking part in a Lakota sun dance.

He shook off his reverie and tucked these details away, saving the bundle of memories, knowing they would accompany him during this difficult day. He looked back at Zac and gave a nod, a silent assurance that they were in this together, carrying Nathan home in the most meaningful way they could.

Zac's expression was serious, contemplative. It wasn't his first experience with death. His grandmother Ahnah and aunt Uki were gone. Ben had no idea whether the ten-year-old Zac was ever told the distressing circumstances; he'd never asked. Now, Zac was learning from Ben's actions and the elder's words, participating in a tradition that stretched across centuries of Navajo culture. Ben knew that this experience would shape him, too. The two made eye contact, then Ben turned to Clarence with a nod. It was time.

With each step toward the open grave, Ben reminded himself that it was not an end. The Diné believed in an afterlife, that we would meet our ancestors again in the Fourth World. He would hold that hope for Nathan, that the young man would soon see his beloved grandmother again.

Ben knelt beside the grave, the smell of freshly turned dirt mingling with juniper. Elder Benally chanted softly in

Navajo as a breeze stirred the fine red dust. Ben felt the rhythm of the prayers connect to his own heartbeat. He laid a folded blanket at the head of the grave; two men from the tribe gently placed Nathan's wrapped body inside. The small gathering stood in a solemn half-circle, the two women humming a mournful song, a young man softly beating a hand drum.

As the grave was filled in, the wind carried the elder's chant across the land, lifting it over the low mesas and letting it fall back with the grace of the offering. Ben absorbed the cadence and the tones, absorbing Nathan's presence in every note and every step of the ceremony.

With bowed head, Ben offered a silent prayer—a thankfulness for knowing Nathan, for their paths that had crossed and intertwined, and for the way forward the family must now travel without him. The silence around them was vast, filled only with the whisper of wind and the echo of the soft voices.

He helped tamp the earth, each press a reminder of the finality humans face. Community members stood nearby, offering their quiet support, acknowledging his willingness to embrace their customs and honor Nathan's life in this way.

The remains of the women's song wove through his thoughts, an ancient melody of departure and return. Ben noted the symbolism: though he'd lived most of his life away from New Mexico, his adopted life blended into something that now felt complete. The ceremony's echoes lingered in haunting harmony.

In the end, as much as Ben had seen this ceremony as an obligation, he saw it ultimately as an honor—a way to show love that transcended even family ties.

The air stilled, the dust settled. Ben rose, his movements deliberate and respectful, knowing that they had given Nathan the gift of belonging to both the earth and to memory. He took a deep breath as the burden lifted and transformed. The empty desert seemed less barren, less alone. It truly was something solid and enduring—the land, the juniper, like Nathan's impact on every life he touched.

After the final blessing, Ben turned to the assembled neighbors, offering his deepest thanks—"Ahéhee' níshłį"—and exchanging polite bows and hand clasps with those who murmured words of appreciation for his care in following the customs. Trini hung back until last, then she wrapped Ben in a warm hug. She dared not show outward grief here at the gravesite, but he understood. He knew what she was telling him.

Heading back to where his truck waited, Zac walked in silence, brow furrowed and hands thrust deep into his jacket pockets. Ben glanced over, seeing so much of himself in his son's serious contemplation. He knew these days had deeply affected Zac in ways that were profound, ways the boy did not yet fully understand.

Standing at the door to his truck, Ben took one last look back at the cemetery. The land beyond was expansive and open, the way Nathan's memory would be, stretching endlessly into their future.

He settled into the driver's seat, the door's creak breaking the afternoon stillness. Zac slipped into the passenger side, his spirit quieter than usual. Ben started the truck but didn't drive right away. He looked straight ahead, letting the horizon fill his view.

He thought of Julie, of her support and love, and the promise he had made to her to keep Nathan's memory vibrant and alive. Ben's biggest regret was that he'd not spent more time with Nathan. With both boys. Life was short, people said. In this case, far too short.

He put the truck in gear and began the slow journey back toward Gallup, where they would stop for some lunch, although he wasn't sure either of them felt like eating. The drive ahead was long, but Ben felt steady. They were going home, taking Nathan with them in every way that mattered. The family they had become was untraditional but he wouldn't have it any other way.

Zac remained silent, eyes fixed out the window, watching the landscape blur past. At least now his mood was more reflective than angry. The world outside seemed vast and unknown, yet also strangely familiar. It was the world Nathan had belonged to and the world that would continue to shape them all.

As they picked up speed, Ben heard the soft rustle of the breeze in his mind, saw the simple marker silhouetted against the deep blue sky. Peace settled around them like a protective embrace, urging them onward.

Chapter 17

Julie looked up from her notes to realize there was daylight showing through the kitchen window. It was one of those mornings when she'd awakened in darkness, her mind spinning with ideas about her recent research. She got up to reheat the kettle for some tea, standing at the window while she waited, noticing for the first time that the sky was filled with colorful orbs, hundreds of them.

It struck her that they were in the midst of the Albuquerque Balloon Fiesta and it actually was the big deal that the news people were making it out to be. As if being pulled by a magnet, she stepped out to the sidewalk, then the grassy berm beside the building. Now she could hear them, the intermittent blasts of the burners as pilots guided their colorful aircraft to various altitudes.

Should she rush inside and wake Ben and Zac to see

the spectacle? But something held her in place, fascinated, until she heard her tea kettle and realized she'd left their door standing open.

"Hey," said Ben. He was standing at the stove, wearing pajama pants, lifting the noisy kettle from the burner.

"Sorry, didn't mean for that to wake you up." She walked into his arms and held him for a long minute. Yesterday had been an emotionally draining one for him. "There's quite a show going on outside, if you want to take a look."

"I'm not dressed for it," he said with a smile, although he did stare out the window. "What are you doing up so early?"

"Brain buzzing, couldn't sleep after about five."

"Still researching your story?"

"Oh, no. That's been over and done for days, although I'm still getting congratulatory notes from colleagues in far-flung places. It's fun, but kind of strange, too." She set her tea mug beside the computer on the dining table. "I've been trying to figure out who would have come after Raven, what enemy would follow her all the way here. It doesn't make a lot of sense, yet we know the tampering with her brakes was very much intentional."

"I'm thankful you have the resources and contacts to track down this kind of thing," he said, returning from the bedroom and pulling a long-sleeved tee over his head.

"I wish there was more. None of my leads have amounted to anything yet. What's on your agenda for the day?"

"I need to have the difficult talk with Sandy Black, let him know the police are sniffing around. I don't know that I'll be able to report for the job right away, like he wanted.

And what if Herrera decides to—" He made a motion to indicate his wrists being cuffed together.

"Ben. Do not even go there. You are innocent, a hundred percent, and we know it. Someone else did this awful thing."

"As they say, prisons are full of innocent people."

His timing couldn't have been worse. Zac was standing in the doorway.

Julie caught the alarm on his face. "Oh, sweetie, your dad didn't mean that. We'll find the answer and everything will be fine."

But the teen turned on his heel and stomped into the bathroom.

Ben turned his eyes toward the ceiling. "That went well. God, when will I learn to keep my mouth shut?"

"Neither of us are accustomed to having 'little ears' around the house," she whispered. "It'll be okay."

"Other than research, what's your plan?" he asked, pulling out two bagels for the toaster.

"Thought I'd drive over to the new house, see how the contractor's doing. Unless you'd rather handle that?"

"Let me see how it goes with Sandy. And I was thinking I might convince Zac to take in a movie. Gotta find out what's playing."

"Or, get the question about schools answered," she suggested. "At some point, the adults will need to make the final call on that."

Ben nodded. She could tell he was stalling, and she understood. Zac was hurting and trying to push him toward a decision about school wasn't helping. Maybe they should talk about letting him sit out a year. But his senior year? That would be rough.

An hour later the guys had left the apartment, somewhat disappointed that the balloons had finished their flights and were no longer in sight. Julie's attention returned to the notes she'd made about Raven and the Iditarod. She had traced some leads back to the dogsled business, and people's vague answers left her curious. Why was everyone being so enigmatic? What was she missing?

She went back to email and opened one of the congratulatory messages about her Florida article, quickly scanning the words. They should have filled her with pride, but she couldn't focus. Too much going on. Too much pulling her attention elsewhere. She bit her lip, dropping the subject of her successful story and turning back to the murder.

What had happened to get Raven killed? The mention of her Iditarod participation kept swirling in Julie's thoughts, relentless as a storm. Her journalistic instincts sensed something more beneath the surface, beyond what people were telling her. The race was more than a friendly competition. Ben and Julie had discovered that on their trip to Alaska a few years ago, when he first learned of Zac's existence. Raven had been immersed in raising dogs and racing, and Julie had a gut feeling that the dogsled people had been hiding something, even then.

Raven's entry in the Iditarod this year seemed at first like an odd footnote. She didn't even live in Alaska anymore. But the more Julie turned it over, the more it felt like a missing puzzle piece. She went back through her notes from one of her phone calls yesterday, remembering the careful way the dogsledding company owner in Alaska talked, confirming Raven's involvement but being vague about the details.

"Was there a reason the woman didn't want to talk to me?" Julie murmured aloud, tapping her pen on her notepad. The dots were there, waiting to be connected.

Okay, take a breath and switch topics. Maybe something will clear up.

What about Seattle, Raven's tattoo business? A response from a Seattle contact caught her eye, and she paused. They'd simply pointed her to online sources she already knew about, the news that a competitor in the tattoo business had come to town and was doing his best to run Raven out. But to kill her? And to send someone nearly a thousand miles away to track her down and kill her … that seemed a bit of a stretch.

But someone coming all the way from Alaska was an even bigger stretch. Raven simply wasn't that much of a threat, in either of those instances. *So, what am I missing?*

Julie stared at the list of names tied to the race, her notes about those breeders and mushers she'd spoken to. And, yes, she understood why they might have been hesitant to say much to an outsider like herself. But still, wouldn't someone among them want the answers to Raven's death?

I have to be getting closer. She jotted down a few questions that came to mind. Maybe some follow-up calls would yield a straight answer. This time she wouldn't let them slip away without something more concrete.

"Dog sledding, the tattoo business, or … what if one of Raven's activism projects had gone too far. What if there are connections between them all?" she whispered, almost amazed at the potential mess unraveling in front of her.

Maybe it was time to push the Alaska angle even harder. It would be helpful if one of her Seattle contacts could put her in touch with someone in Anchorage. And she had to ask herself why she wasn't leaping right in to ask the Takanni family—they would surely know if Raven had enemies. Maybe? But something told her they would simply close ranks and let Ben take the blame for this. Perhaps even gladly.

Her notebook was a chaotic mess, with lines crisscrossed and thoughts filling the margins. But to Julie, it was perfect order—a map showing her the way forward. In the back of her mind, another question burned: Raven had enemies, but how was any of it tied to the crash?

Julie sat back, exhaling deeply as she looked around the cluttered table. She smiled briefly, knowing she was close. Her next move could prove to be the right one.

Chapter 18

Ben thought Zac's mood had improved a bit since yesterday. He knew the nature of grieving was always an ebb and flow—moments of complete normality, overridden by almost physical pain that went right to the heart. And the trip to Gallup, seeing Nathan laid to rest, had been especially wearing on both of them. Funerals didn't always bring closure, but they did provide a step toward acceptance of the loss.

They pulled up in front of the place that would soon be their new home. Ben recognized the contractor's logo on the side of a white F-250 crew cab in the driveway, and a plumber's vehicle sat at the curb. Two men in coveralls had some lengths of pipe on their shoulders. The kitchen and bath work must be well underway.

Julie had spoken with the general contractor on the

phone, several times, but this was Ben's first time to meet him in person.

"Erik Brown," the man said, holding out a hand as Ben and Zac walked into the entry hall.

Ben registered a lanky guy who was only a couple inches shorter than himself, sandy blonde hair in need of a trim since it kept falling across his forehead, blue eyes, and calluses that revealed this wasn't a suit who owned a business. He did much of the work himself.

"The rough-in plumbing is pretty well done. All the old pipe is replaced with the best we have now. Cabinetry will arrive tomorrow, fixtures within a week." Erik turned toward the living and dining rooms. "Now, I believe your wife said all the old hardwood flooring stays?"

"That's what she tells me, too," Ben said with a smile. "Décor is totally her department."

Erik met Zac's gaze. "You can choose your own paint color for your bedroom, if you like. You'll need to tell me which rooms are whose, and then take a look at the color charts."

Ben could tell Zac hadn't a clue. "Is it okay if we take the color charts home so Julie can help us with that?"

"Sure. I get it. Moms always have the last say." He didn't catch Zac's flinch, but when Ben softly told him the boy's mother had recently passed away, Erik did have the good grace to apologize and offer condolences.

Ben took the offered paint color chart, trying to notice details about the progress of the work so he could report to Julie.

"Sorry, that was awkward," he said to Zac ten minutes later when they climbed back into Ben's truck.

"I'm almost getting used to it," Zac said. But his stare

was vacant out the side window.

Ben started the truck and steered out of the quiet neighborhood. He truly did think they would like it here.

"So. Next up would either be a meeting with my new boss, or another drive-by at the school you'll be attending. I'm thinking the school will be more interesting. We can get a supply list and start the enrollment process."

"I thought you were saying I might go to the one closer to the apartment."

"We'll see. It seems like we'll be in the new house well before Christmas break, so the school on this side of town kind of makes more sense."

"Whatever." And the mood was back.

As Julie had said this morning, at some point the adults would need to make some basic decisions on Zac's behalf, so Ben drove to the Albuquerque High campus. They walked into the admin building where they'd visited a few days ago, but the counselor who met them this time was not the middle-aged woman who tended to fuss too much. This was a male who seemed impossibly young to Ben, but he used enough PhD-speak to pass muster.

"So, Zac, I understand you'll probably be joining us pretty soon, so I thought maybe we could spend a couple hours together? I'd love for you to sit in on some of the classes you'd be taking this semester. Maybe stay for lunch?"

Zac gave the vacant teen stare that indicated he didn't care because he knew the decision wasn't really his. Ben wanted to reassure him, but it seemed better to go with the flow right now and deal with the aftermath later. Who knew—maybe Zac would love this place.

"I have a meeting at my own workplace," Ben offered, "and I know Zac will be a lot less bored here than tagging along with me."

"Lunch is over at one o'clock. You can plan on coming back any time after that," the counselor said.

"You've got my number if you need it in the meantime." Ben couldn't believe how relieved he felt when he walked out, leaving Zac under someone else's watchful eye for a while.

It wasn't that he didn't want to spend loads of time with his son, not that at all. But the moods had begun to weigh on all of them. He phoned Sandy Black when he reached the parking lot and received an immediate invitation to pop by.

He'd always found Albuquerque a fairly easy city to get around in, with the major streets mostly following a north-south or east-west grid. He remembered where Sandy's office was, although it seemed the trees had grown, and a few new buildings had sprouted during the years Ben was away from New Mexico.

"Ben, I'm so sorry for your family's loss and for everything you're going through," Sandy said, ushering him into his private office and closing the door.

Ben had only spoken briefly with Sandy since the afternoon he arrived here in the city and they'd met for that drink, a time that seemed unbelievably carefree and long ago. He let out a long sigh and started with the speech he'd rehearsed. "Well, I'm not sure where to start, but there's a lot more to it."

* * *

Julie stretched and felt something pop in her shoulder. The hours of online and phone research were way more sedentary than she'd realized. At her newspaper job, there had been plenty of that, but always interspersed with a rush trip for an interview, refreshing her hair and makeup for a meeting or a camera. Sitting on her butt, on a hard dining chair in a tiny apartment, was taking a toll on her body. She stood and did a few yoga moves to loosen up.

Enough of this, she thought. She could wait on phone calls and check email on her phone, and still get out for some fresh air. Lunch and a walk. There was a nice park a couple blocks away, so she grabbed an apple and some string cheese from the fridge, stuck her phone and keys in her pockets, and headed out.

She'd forgotten what a perfect place New Mexico was to live, this time of year. With crisp, chilly mornings that morphed into warm afternoons, there was nothing hazy here. And no alligator would suddenly poke its snout out of the foliage.

She watched some kids and their mothers at the playground while she munched on her apple, peeking at her phone now and then to see if her contact in Seattle had tried to reach out. She'd been digging deep into some of Raven's protest activities, looking for names or events that might suggest she'd made an enemy or two in the process of being so vocal. Nothing jumped out, so now Julie was hoping a contact from Seattle, a woman her age who'd worked at the same New York news outlet and then moved on, would know of someone with an inside track.

Most of Raven's activism days seemed to have been when she still lived in Alaska, and that was most likely where Julie would need to find leads. But Seattle might be prime territory as well. She fumed a bit at the silence on her phone, then chided herself. Here she was, in a new city, a beautiful park, beginning a new adventure in life, and she was back to her old ways of pushing for the story, for new leads.

Except this time, it wasn't about getting a story, she reminded herself. It was about saving Ben's reputation, maybe his life.

She tossed her apple core into a trash bin and headed back to the apartment. Her car was one of two in the parking lot this time of day. This was a working-class building, where ninety percent of the residents left every morning and returned after five. A flutter of white on her windshield caught her attention, a flyer of some kind. She walked over and plucked it off.

It wasn't a flyer. This was a sheet of plain, ordinary office paper, folded in half. She opened it and saw handwritten words: *Stop poking around!*

What? Her pulse leapt and her gaze raced around, taking in the parking lot, the building, the storage facility and homes across the street. Two cars cruised by, slowing for the light at the corner. Otherwise, nothing moved.

But whoever left this note had not done it randomly. The message wasn't generic, and Julie realized all at once how much time she'd spent in the apartment alone. She searched her memory to recall if the note had been under her wiper blade when she left for her walk to the park. She didn't think so.

So, this person, whoever had delivered the note, must have been watching as she walked out her door and left the property. They might have waited until she left, then broken into the apartment and gone through her notes.

"God, Julie, stop it!" Her racing thoughts might be true, but she could simply be turning paranoid.

She stared at the front door of the apartment, forty feet away. *Okay, I have to check this out. But if the door isn't one-hundred percent the way I left it, I am outta here so fast.*

She pulled her phone from her back pocket, ready to hit the Emergency Call button if anything at all looked wrong. But the front door was locked, and when she stepped over to the kitchen window and peered in, she could see nothing out of place.

With her phone gripped in one hand, she pulled out her keys and cautiously opened the door. Her computer and notes were on the table, exactly as she'd left them. She quickly checked the other rooms, finding nothing out of place.

Okay, I am being paranoid. Someone had either overheard a conversation, they'd found a way to spy on her online searches, or they were guessing what she was up to. There were other times in her journalism career where she'd poked a beehive. She'd survived those and she would survive this one.

She found a plastic zipper bag in the kitchen and dropped the sinister note into it. If anything came of it, odds were the only fingerprints on it would be hers and the person who'd issued the threat. That person *would* be caught.

She sat down at her computer, putting on her brave face, and went back to her last search. But her mind wouldn't stop going over the details. The deadly act against Raven had surely come from out of state. Raven had no ties to New Mexico, other than Ben and the kids.

But someone here in Albuquerque was orchestrating things. The note. The tampered brake line. Those were real, and dangerous. They'd come here to get Raven, and now they also knew where Julie was.

She picked up her phone and called Ben, needing to hear his voice. "Hey, what are you guys up to?"

"I'm at Sandy Black's office at the moment, kinda in the middle of something. Zac's getting a guided tour of Albuquerque High." He paused a moment too long. "Everything all right?"

No. "Yeah, probably." She was standing at the kitchen window now, watching her car. No one approached it or showed an interest. "I'm gonna get out of here for a while. Call me if you need anything."

That was lame, she realized. Ben was busy, and his meeting with Sandy was too important to interrupt with a girly 'I'm-scared' message. She picked up her computer, jamming it and all her notes into her messenger bag. Grabbing her purse and keys, she carefully locked up, checking and rechecking the door. It didn't hit her until she got into her car—what if the person who left the note had also tampered with *her* brakes?

Chapter 19

B en, it was fine. I went out to the parking lot and carefully checked the ground under my car for drips of brake fluid. I even moved it and got back out so I could see my parking space well. Nothing looked wrong, so I went for a drive to test it further." She was beginning to wish she hadn't showed him the threatening note.

"Julie … this could have turned serious." Ben's face bore stern lines she'd rarely seen before.

"Hon, I checked it out. Drove through the whole residential area around here at twenty miles an hour, watched my dashboard for warning lights. Nothing was wrong." She laid a gentle hand on his arm. "I ventured farther, but not onto the freeway. I'll take the car in tomorrow and have a mechanic put it up on the rack, to be sure."

He gave her a sideways look, his mouth a straight line.

Zac walked out of the bathroom and Julie's smile perked up. "So, I want to hear about your day. I guess you got the chance to check out your new school?"

"It was okay. What's for dinner?"

"I picked up a huge salad at the deli, and there's fried chicken to go with."

Zac smiled—he'd always been a kid who was open to salads and veggies—then he turned to the sofa and switched on the TV.

Ben followed her into the kitchen, his earlier worry eased.

"So, tell me about your meeting with Sandy. Everything okay there?"

"It's great," he admitted. "Sandy told me to take all the time I need before reporting to the job. It's a newly created position, so it's not like there's a backlog of work already. We talked a lot about the needs at the various pueblos, the ways I can be of help. I'm hoping we can expand on the behavioral health aspects of the agency and create some new programs."

Julie spread the chicken pieces from the market on a baking sheet and put it in the oven to warm while Ben looked through their selection of salad dressings in the fridge.

"Sandy also gave me the name of an attorney," he admitted, not meeting her eyes as he rummaged for forks in the silverware drawer. "In case I need one."

"You told him what's been going on, with the police interviews?"

"Felt I had to. I mean, how would it be for my brand-new employer to see my name on the news?"

"Oh, Ben, do you think it will come to that?"

"I sincerely hope not. But you said it yourself, the police have made up their minds. I'm sure they're gathering their evidence right now."

Julie realized the TV show had been muted. "Let's talk more about this later."

They carried their plates to the living room and started a movie of Zac's choosing, an action-adventure thing with lots of explosions and actors who performed impossible leaps and kicks. Julie's mind kept wandering as she ate her salad, and by the time everyone was finished with the meal and she'd brought out a box of chocolate chip cookies, she was more than ready to get back to the notes and papers she'd left spread out over the dining table.

Someone was scared. Scared enough to have done away with Raven and now to threaten Julie's own research into the factors that led to the tampering. She had to stay ahead, to figure this out before the next threat arrived. She took the note, smoothing it against the table with a defiant smile. It hadn't worked. They hadn't scared her off. But she had to wonder—the person who left the note on her car, how had they known she was 'poking around' and how did they know her location?

Her internet connection was supposed to be secure, her phone one of the most difficult to hack. Unless this was some sort of master criminal with connections in high places, how would they even know what she was working on? Neither Raven's tattoo business nor her role in the dogsled racing world seemed important enough to draw that caliber of criminal mind.

But the protests—could there be something so detrimental, something Raven knew, that a mega corporation would pay to take her out of the picture? Earlier, Julie had discovered several rants on Raven's social media pages. She brought those up on her computer screen and reread them. A link included in one of the posts reminded her of an old friend who still worked at the *Seattle Times*. Sure enough, she found an article about pipeline protests that included his byline.

Did she still have his number? She picked up her phone and scrolled through her lengthy contacts list. There. Jeffrey Lemogh. She tapped his number, wondering whether it was still valid, and then he picked up.

"Jeff? Julie Conlin here." She got up and stepped into the kitchen to get away from the blaring sound of the television.

They went through a long five minutes of gosh-how-are-you and catching up on job changes and moves before she got to the topic at hand.

"Raven Takanni … refresh my memory?"

Julie went into the highlights of the various things Raven had been involved in. He remembered the pipeline protest story. It was one of those that spanned news audiences in Alaska, Canada, and Washington state. "Ms. Takanni was recently killed in a car crash, which is being investigated as suspicious. This happened in New Mexico."

"Wow, that's pretty far away."

"Yeah, and she'd only been in the state about twenty-four hours when it happened. I'm looking for any kind of connection to her previous activities, some motive as to why someone would have followed her here and tampered with her car."

"Let me … ah, okay, here are my background notes on the story I ran."

She could hear pages flipping and pictured the spiral

notebooks carried by so many reporters who wanted something on paper, in addition to recordings or phone calls.

"Hm, I'm remembering the interview now. Raven Takanni stepped forward to speak with me as one of those protests was winding down. The guy who had spearheaded it that day had already left. Ms. Takanni gave me enough facts and figures to flesh out the piece, but I didn't get any sense that she was a major instigator. After I talked with her, I made a call to the number I was given as the headquarters for the movement—I'm using the term loosely. The woman on the phone verified that Raven's name was on their call list, you know, someone willing to show up at the day and time, carry a sign around, and shout the slogans. But she definitely wasn't a prime organizer or anyone that important there."

Julie chewed on her lower lip for a moment, considering. "Doesn't sound at all like she would be worth following for a thousand miles, or that killing her would stop the protests or benefit anyone."

"Exactly."

She thanked Jeff for the information and hung up, pondering. If Raven's various protest involvements amounted to nothing, it seemed to leave the tattoo competitor as the likely one to get rid of her. But, really? Driving someone out of business was a far cry from killing them. None of this was making much sense.

Raven had put in a lot of years to build her tattoo business in Seattle after her shop in Anchorage shut down. Would she willingly abandon it, when she had seemingly found her place in a city large enough to support her? Perhaps she'd done something to this business competitor, to retaliate for the vandalism she'd claimed was their fault. Tracking her down could be payback.

Julie put the kettle on the stove and got out her favorite mug for tea. While she was pawing through the cupboard for the teabags, she sensed movement at her side.

Ben edged in beside her and placed a gentle kiss on her neck. "Movie not exactly to your liking?" he teased.

"Too preoccupied," she admitted. "I can still hear it though. Did all the death-defying action wear thin for you too?"

"A bit, yeah. I'll take a cup of tea, if we have green?"

"We do."

She prepared two mugs and shared the gist of the phone call with the Seattle reporter. "Did Raven say much to you about was else was going on in her life? I'm struggling to find anything that angered someone enough to kill her."

Ben gave it a minute's thought and shook his head. "Not really. She was pretty upset about this other tattoo operation coming into her neighborhood. It's one of those outfits with branches in different places, a personable founder who made a name for himself on YouTube and social media and then got a TV reality show. So, yeah, I can see where his shop could easily overwhelm hers."

"But that would be a reason for her to kill him, not the other way around. Not that I think Raven would have actually—"

"No, I get it. She had a temper."

"Ben, I'm sorry. I don't mean to—"

"Shh, shh. I appreciate everything you're doing to get to the bottom of this." He picked up the mug she'd prepared for him, dipping the teabag several times.

"Among those she had her differences with, it seems

to come down to this business competitor or someone involved in the Iditarod. Do you think Raven had decided to go back to Alaska—a natural choice if her business in Washington went under? And maybe she'd planned to ramp up the competition in the dog sled race? Which would reheat that old rivalry. Someone might not like the competition, and suddenly things get … difficult."

"I have no idea. We might learn more when we talk to her family again."

"Not an easy conversation." She took a tentative sip of her tea.

Ben sighed. "I think I'll drive up to Tewa tomorrow. Sandy suggested it after I told him about the police and how much we've got weighing on us right now. Said a day at the pueblo might help me clear my head."

"I agree. A change of scenery and the chance to see your aunts, without a huge family gathering like last time— it might be just the thing."

"And maybe I'll take Zac along. He's not ready to settle into a new school yet. The counselor and I agreed on that, at least not until after Raven's funeral, which will be in Alaska. The kid is at loose ends here in the apartment. This'll give us the chance to talk, father-son, and maybe the elders at the pueblo will have some wisdom that will help both of us."

Julie reached out and took his hand. "Sounds perfect."

Chapter 20

Ben stepped from the car, inhaling the high desert layers of scent—sage, piñon, and woodsmoke riding the chilly gusts. The familiar mountains stood silent, their presence providing comfort amid his troubled thoughts. Aunt Zena had promised them lunch, and Ben wanted to get an early start, to spend most of the day visiting before they needed to head back to the city.

Voices and the thudding of basketballs could be heard a short distance away. "What do you think, buddy?" he asked, turning to Zac. Ignoring his son's noncommittal shrug, Ben started walking in that direction, assuming correctly that the young man would follow.

They passed between two closely built adobe homes and followed the narrow dirt street to the central plaza where someone had put up a basketball hoop attached to one of the wooden vigas at the front of the post office. Six boys were taking turns at shooting baskets. They took one look at Zac's height and each group shouted for him to join their team.

Across the way, Ben spotted Vicente. His cousin stood near the kiva, posture relaxed but eyes watchful, engaged in conversation with a group of young men. Before Ben got close, he saw a packet change hands, its journey swift and discreet. Ben tucked that observation away and approached the circle, calling out a greeting.

"Hey, Vicente. It's good to see you again." Ben infused his words with warmth, hoping to break the disdainful look he was getting.

So much for their talk under the stars the last time he visited.

Vicente's eyes narrowed, and his response came slow. "Yo, it's Ben. Or should we call you Benson now?" He didn't bother to hide the edge in his voice.

Ben caught the smirks from the other men, and he let his own smile grow, an old habit of weathering storms with calm. "Either one works. I thought I'd come by and catch up, spend a day back at home." He glanced at the younger men, acknowledging them without expecting anything back.

Vicente looked more amused than welcoming. "Old Benson's back. Maybe for good?" He turned to the others. "Watch out, guys, he might be checking on us."

Ben felt the sting but didn't flinch. This was a lifelong story with them—treating him one way when they were alone, completely different when peers were present. "No checking. Just visiting. Things look busy here. How have you been?" He pitched his tone easy and open, keeping the conversation light.

"Been real busy. Getting ready for winter stuff, you know. Deer dances coming up." Vicente stretched, his movements loose and unbothered. "Same as always. Pueblo life. Maybe you remember it."

Ben nodded, keeping the atmosphere from tilting too far. "It's hard to forget. I was telling Julie how much I miss it sometimes." He spoke as if their shared past could bridge the present.

Vicente let the pause stretch, long enough for everyone to feel it. "Must be different from where you've been, out there in the white man's world in Flo-rid-ah." He stretched out the word, making a big deal of it.

Ben leaned in, holding onto his composure. "It's different, all right. But some things are the same no matter where you are." He offered a slow nod, knowing Vicente would understand his meaning but would be likely to toss it back.

Vicente took the bait but twisted it. "Yeah, like when people think they're better 'cause they went away for school." He chuckled, and the others joined. "Or when they come back with the big-city attitude."

Ben heard the challenge clear as a drumbeat. He considered his words with care, aware of all the ears listening. "I'm trying to bring what I know back home. Help where I can." His voice held steady.

The taller of the young men gave Vicente a sideways glance, seeking cues. "I guess you don't need much of that fancy stuff around here, though," the man ventured, looking for approval.

Vicente snorted, smirk broadening. "We've been doing okay without a resident psychologist." His focus snapped back to Ben. "But hey, whatever makes you feel important."

It was the same harassment he'd been dealt through his childhood, but Ben resisted the urge to defend himself, his upbringing, the choices that led him away and back. He stayed in the present moment with these men, a reminder of the deep ties and deeper rifts that time had built. He softened his tone, switching tactics. "Maybe I'll catch the deer dances this year. Zac would enjoy that."

Vicente gave him a long look, and for a second, Ben thought he saw a flicker of something less hostile, something closer to the connection they'd had a few times. But it vanished as Vicente squared his shoulders, reasserting control. "Guess you'll have to wait and see," he said, final and cool. He turned back to the others, a clear signal. The discussion was over.

Ben let the remark settle. "I'll wait," he said softly, barely loud enough for Vicente to hear, and walked away from the kiva.

The comforting scent of roasted chile filled the compact kitchen as Ben and his aunt Dora settled onto the worn chairs, the walls lined with old photographs and memories. Her warm embrace lingered, relieving the tension he'd felt in the plaza. Though her smile radiated welcome, he caught the flicker of worry in her eyes.

"I'm so glad you're here," she said, her voice hinting at something more urgent. She paused, searching his face. "There are things we need to talk about."

He nodded, already anticipating the conversation. "I could sense it's not easy here right now." He reached for the coffee mug in front of him, wrapping his hands around its warmth.

Her expression turned serious, tinged with a sadness he'd seen before but never quite like this. "I don't know what to do about my son. Vicente's got himself in over his head, and he won't listen to us."

Ben waited, allowing the space for her to continue.

"He's running with the wrong people, and I'm afraid it's going to get worse." She glanced down, twisting the edge of her apron between her fingers. "We think he's messing with drugs. Maybe even dealing. People are saying things."

Ben let the words settle between them. He didn't mention the packet changing hands he'd witnessed.

Her eyes met his, confirming what they both feared. "He's so proud to show he's strong and doesn't need anyone. That makes it hard to reach him."

"It sounds like he's under pressure," Ben said softly. "As the eldest, he must feel like everyone expects a lot from him."

Her voice dropped. "It's not only about Vicente. There are other young men, too. Everyone thinks because he's the oldest he should be setting a better example. His father's not here right now. Got a job up near Farmington. He can't help." She looked at Ben, both of them knowing Vicente was a grown man, making his own choices.

Ben took a deep breath, considering his response. "I've seen this in other places. There are ways to help, but it takes time and the right approach. It can't feel like an attack on him."

"That's why we hoped you could get through," she said. "He's jealous of you for leaving, but he listens when you talk about things."

He thought back to his conversations with troubled young people, and although Vicente was now in his forties, the advice was the same. Defenses built from fear and pride often came down, given patience and understanding.

"He does know a lot about the pueblo ways," Ben said, offering an olive branch. "He could turn that into something positive, if he let himself."

She smiled sadly. "I think he's scared. Scared he can't be like his father and uncles. Like you. He'd rather seem tough than to try and fail."

Ben leaned forward, the steam from the coffee rising between them. "I'll do what I can, but we need to be careful. Too much pressure and he'll push back even harder."

She reached across the table, squeezing his hand with a strength that belied her years. "Just be there, Ben. Keep showing up."

They sat in silence for a long moment. "I wish the world was simpler," Dora finally said, a wistful smile breaking through. "Like when you were a kid and would visit for summers. The hardest decision you had was which riverbank to explore."

Ben chuckled, grateful for the brief levity. "Or how to sneak an extra cookie from the kitchen."

She leaned back, the tension in her shoulders easing. "I wish that was all Vicente had to worry about. But things are changing so fast. It's hard to hold on to the old ways and still live in today's world."

"The younger kids have it even tougher," Ben agreed. "At least Vicente had a childhood without all these outside pressures."

"That's why it's so important we don't give up on him. I know it seems like he doesn't care, but he does. We need to help him see a different way." Her eyes held his.

He drained his coffee mug and stood. "I'll be back and we'll work on this."

He thought of Detective Herrera in Albuquerque, and

hoped his promise could be kept.

Outside again, Ben left Dora's cozy home and walked toward the post office, where the basketball game seemed to be winding down.

"Want to see my favorite spot when I was a kid?" he asked Zac.

"Sure." The smile on the boy's face seemed genuine.

Ben tilted his head toward the river and led the way. Red willow and Russian olive lined the banks. The spot where he used to plop down and slide on his bottom, coming to a stop right before his feet hit the water, had worn away and didn't look nearly as thrilling as it used to. But the bend in the river, a hundred yards farther on … that still looked the same.

"I'd bet the fish still hang out there," he told his son. "Next time, we'll give it a try."

They walked on, passing the road that led uphill to one of the cornfields, and Ben told Zac about the times he'd helped Uncle Joe harvest the fat ears of corn.

"One of those times, my cousin was about fourteen, I think. Uncle Joe let him drive the truck—" Ben's voice faltered. Vicente had wrecked the truck, rolling it down an embankment. Not a story for Zac to hear so soon. "Yeah, we had some great memories when we helped out in the fields. Those were fun summers for me here."

Leaving the riverbank, they circled toward the cemetery. Ben had promised Zac a visit to Lorenzo Loretto's grave. The old man had lived to age one-hundred, more or less. No one was exactly sure. Ben's stories of the pueblo's oldest citizen had always intrigued Zac, especially the way Lorenzo treated everything as a gift, including the time Julie had loaned him a favorite poncho, never to get it back.

They stood for a while, Ben recalling and recounting other stories, wondering what Lorenzo would think of the modern grave marker people had chipped in to buy and the small bunch of wildflowers someone had left recently. The gesture touched Ben. And at least Zac was smiling again by the time they continued their walk.

They'd almost reached the edge of pueblo land when Ben checked his watch. "Guess we'd better head back. Aunt Zena makes a terrific lunch."

He could smell the food as they approached her house, and when they stepped inside those heady scents brought back so many memories.

"Benson! Your timing is perfect. Zac, I swear you are taller than you were last week." Zena pulled them into a group hug, and Zac sent a long eye-roll toward Ben, who gave him a wide grin.

She had filled the table with baked squash, venison, and chicken. Two other women emerged from the kitchen, carrying traditional blue corn tortillas and beans. Behind him, Uncle Frank walked in and greeted the visitors heartily. Zac's expression lingered in Ben's mind as he observed his family, seeing how his son took in the tradition. He seemed open, giving Ben hope that the connections would continue to grow stronger in the coming months. They took seats around the table.

"You should have seen Nia at that last corn dance she participated in, when you were a kid," Aunt Dora was saying, laughter filling her words. She appeared not to notice that Vicente hadn't showed up for the meal. "Dressed, you might say … differently, but with all the grace you could want."

"Mom loved the dances," Ben replied, a soft smile accompanying the early memories.

Zac sat between two of his younger cousins. He appeared relaxed, his grief receding for this short time, as if he could exist in this world and his mother's world with equal ease.

Vicente walked in and took a chair, his earlier challenge toward Ben now turned into shared remembrance. "The kids will all have to dance this year. Even the new ones." His look to Zac was full of encouragement. Ben could tell he was high. Decided to let it go, for now.

The room erupted into laughter, and for a moment, Ben felt the joy outpace the mourning. It was a brief escape from the heaviness that had pressed down on them. The stories flowed as freely as the food, and Ben let the unity wash over him, even as he knew it would be temporary. The knowledge didn't dampen the relief he felt, seeing Zac absorb a piece of this heritage, forming connections in ways Ben had long struggled with.

The meal ended, the mood congenial. Aunt Dora caught Ben's eye and followed along as he and Zac started walking toward his truck. He tossed Zac the keys and suggested he go on ahead. Then he stepped aside to take Dora's hand. "I'll start looking into what we can do," he promised quietly. "I know some people who might be able to help."

She nodded, a flicker of hope crossing her features. "Your grandfather always said nothing is too hard if we face it together."

He smiled. "Then that's what we'll do."

"Come back tomorrow," she said, "and the day after that. Just keep showing up."

Ben laughed, a good-natured way of letting her

know that he couldn't drive up here every day, but he'd do his best. As he climbed into his truck, he thought of Sandy Black and the work they'd done together in other communities. Maybe the new programs would be of real help to puebloans like Vicente. He would talk to Sandy about it as soon as he could.

Chapter 21

Sandy studied Ben for a moment, as if diagnosing a fever or reading symptoms. "This sounds like more than your cousin."

Ben's shoulders sagged slightly. "It is. The more I see, the more I realize drug use is pervasive and growing. His mother said Vicente showed up high at a family ceremony. I knew he had to be getting the stuff somewhere, maybe bringing it to the other kids. I didn't want to believe my cousin would be that guy. But then I witnessed a drug exchange."

Sandy listened carefully, leaning back in his chair, nodding at Ben's words. "This isn't your fault."

"I know, but … I'm supposed to help. This is my own family…" Ben trailed off, searching for the right words. "I feel like I'm letting them all down."

"These things are complicated, Ben. Don't take on more guilt than you deserve."

"Maybe, but if we can't do something we're going to lose another generation. Before lunch at Tewa yesterday, I tried talking to him. Tried getting him to open up again. He's too proud, or stubborn."

"Sometimes the people we love the most are the hardest to reach." Sandy's eyes held such gentle kindness.

Ben took a deep breath. "What if he doesn't listen until it's too late?"

"I think you know that these crises need more than one person and more than one plan," Sandy said, as if reading from a manual. "Let's focus on what you *can* do."

Ben nodded, absorbing Sandy's words. His mind flickered back to simpler times, the sun-warmed adobe buildings of the pueblo, the sound of the river, the deep blue of the sky, and long summers spent with his grandmother. They hadn't been free of trouble then, but at least he hadn't felt so responsible for fixing things.

"Remember that you're not the same kid you were back then," Sandy added, pulling him back to the present. "You have training, experience, resources."

"I don't want to be the outsider who shows up and tells everyone what's wrong."

"You're not an outsider, Ben," Sandy insisted. "You're someone who understands both sides. That's why you're in the position to make a difference."

Ben absorbed the words, weighing Sandy's reassurances against his internal struggle. The memory of Vicente's laughter, once teasing and genuine, now seemed filled with mocking echoes.

"Tell me what you think I should do."

Sandy leaned forward, resting his elbows on his knees.

"First off, remember your training. This is what you do so well. Keep talking to Vicente. But don't rely only on words. Get him involved, make him part of the solution."

"*If* he'll participate. Why does this feel so different when it's family, not a client?"

"Look at the bigger picture. We can set up programs that can reach him indirectly. Involve others. Sometimes—oftentimes—people take direction better from someone they aren't related to."

Ben nodded. "We'll have to start small, build from there. Peer counseling, educational outreach, cultural programs—use all of them together."

The strategies unfolded in Ben's mind, practical and ambitious at the same time. He realized Sandy was right; it wasn't about imposing one perfect solution. It was about trying many possible approaches.

Sandy was watching his expression as it changed. "Remember that you have colleagues, friends who want to help. You don't have to do this alone."

"You're right. I think I'm feeling the pressure because this is my home territory. I need to do it right." He stood and reached across the desk to shake his friend's hand. "Thanks, Sandy. This helped."

"Ben … How are *you* doing? I mean, what we talked about before …"

"I'm going with the idea that no news is good news. The police aren't telling us anything."

Sandy nodded, his mouth in a firm line. "I want you to call me if you need to. And talk to Marguerite Ortiz, introduce yourself and let her know what's going on."

The lawyer Sandy had recommended. He still needed to call her. "I can't thank you enough for this."

"Anytime," Sandy replied, a smile breaking through his serious demeanor. "We're in this together, Ben. We'll find a way."

Ben left the office with the fresh reminder of the police in his head. Would life ever settle down?

Chapter 22

Ben eyed the boxes stacked along the wall, many of them in states of half-birth—tops open and flaps unfurled, waiting for life in the new house. He pulled a sealed box toward him, brushing dust off the marker-scrawl that looked suspiciously like Julie's. "If you ask me, it says 'Miscellaneous.' Same as the last two."

She laughed, pulling a cutter from her pocket. "My handwriting's not *that* terrible, is it?" She handed over the blade, a sly look in her eyes.

"Let's see what's in these before we dig into any others," she added, settling onto the floor beside him.

Ben sliced the tape and folded the top open. A mound of bubble wrap peeked out, taunting them with the promise of fragile treasures. "I'm betting picture frames. Maybe a flower vase."

"Or last year's tax forms," Julie said. "As fast as I was throwing stuff in boxes before we got the U-Haul, anything could be pretty much anywhere."

Ben paused and glanced around the cluttered room. "No point in truly unpacking until we're in the new place."

"I know," Julie said, "but you have to admit, it's not fun digging through every box when you're looking for a pair of scissors."

"You mean like these?" He pulled a pair from the bubble wrap, holding them up with a smug grin.

"Okay, okay. You win this one." She shook her head. "We should do a better job of labeling things."

"*We?* I think most of these labels are yours, my love. Besides, what's the fun in that?" He leaned back, crossing his legs and watching her reach into the box. He marveled at her efficiency, the way she seemed to coax each item free with minimal effort. "Deciphering them brings mystery to our lives."

"Don't we have enough of that already?" Julie handed him a photo frame, carefully wrapped and intact. "It might be nice to have one predictable thing. Like finding your office supplies before Christmas."

"Exactly. That was the mission for today. I'm hoping to at least get my basic setup ready at IHS." Before anything worse hits the fan. But he didn't say it.

A smile lit her face. "We've got to be close. I'm not sure I can survive another one of these epic moves without better organization. Without my special conditioner, my hair has been staticky since we got to this climate."

"I love the static," he said. "It's kind of your trademark."

Julie waved off the compliment, though she clearly appreciated it. "But seriously, I'm ready for some nesting time. I want us to be able to relax, not feel like we're in a storage unit."

Ben's eyes softened. "We can work on that. We have to pace ourselves. It's what, a few more weeks now?"

"Looks like we'll be in before Thanksgiving. I stopped by today, talked with the cabinet installers—those kitchen cabinets are *so* gorgeous, by the way. Even better in person than in the photos." She stuffed the bubble wrap back into the box she'd finished searching. "And I went by the showroom where Erik wanted me to pick out fixtures— faucets, shower heads, toilets, and sinks. Luckily, everything was in stock and they've set it all aside for us."

Ben looked at the object in her hand, a hand-carved wooden flute. It had been a gift from the Lakota chief he'd helped in South Dakota.

She set it on the shelf and turned to him. "I thought you were going to learn to play this thing?"

"Unfortunately, I think it's spent more time packed than played. I should get busy."

"It's never too late," Julie said. "Unless you want to tackle that first." She gestured to a tower of "Miscellaneous" boxes by the couch.

"Leave those. I think this might be the right box. But why is it so heavy?" Ben wondered, hefting the box as he lifted it to the coffee table.

"If memory serves, your professional journals and reference books are at the bottom," Julie replied. She flopped back onto the couch, exhaling with a sense of satisfaction. "At least this time we won't have to haul things cross-country again. I don't even want to think about that long drive."

"Yeah, that was intense." Ben ran a hand through his hair. He lowered his voice, mindful of Zac in his bedroom.

"And it's going to get more intense until we've dealt with Raven's family and get Zac's things moved here. But for this moment, right now we've got some downtime. We can actually catch up with each other instead of just passing through."

Julie met his gaze, her eyes softening. "That sounds wonderful. I've missed you, you know."

"Right back at you." But he pointed toward his son's room, a reminder that they weren't truly alone.

Ben pulled items from the box: his address book, a box of pens, two reams of copy paper (even though the IHS office would surely supply that), his favorite desk pad, calendar with dates marked that were now irrelevant, stapler, scissors, colored markers.

"What's this?" He held up a wrapped package, expecting Julie to admit to an act of sneaky gifting, a surprise for him to open at the office on his first day of work.

But her face had turned stark white.

"Jules?"

"It's like that other one," she whispered. Julie wrapped her arms around herself, fighting the shiver that raised goosebumps.

The box was about six inches long, three wide, and two inches tall, and the paper was the same as that used on the envelope containing the photo they'd discovered earlier.

"Promise me you didn't wrap this up, as a gag gift or something." But he knew by her expression that wasn't the case.

"The only thing I can think is that Sally helped me pack some of these boxes, the neighbor."

He remembered people pitching in to help them organize and move. And that might explain how someone had a photo of Zac. And maybe they'd wanted the gifts to be a surprise. "We'll open it and find out," he declared, ripping the paper off in one quick move.

Inside the box was a carved alligator. Its wooden surface gleamed, an artifact that tied them back to their old lives.

"It's beautiful work," Julie said softly, her voice a mix of awe and repulsion.

It *might* be a toy—possibly one of Zac's, abandoned long ago—but it was realistic and high quality enough to have been a gallery or gift store purchase, not something a kid could afford.

"Zac! Can you come out here a minute?" But when Zac appeared and Ben held up the alligator, he backed away. "I take it this isn't yours?"

"No way. Sorry, but I never did love the wildlife of Florida. I wouldn't have played with that thing. Give me a polar bear any day."

"Okay, thanks. We needed to know." Ben set the alligator on the coffee table and waited until Zac had left the room again. "Someone is playing games."

"What should we do?"

"I don't think we can rule out a prankster. It's possible one of the friends who helped us pack thought these *gifts* would be fun surprises for us. With all that's happened since we got here, we're sensitive."

"Maybe that's it. I can call Sally, pretend I'm thanking her for the gift, see what she says." She set the carved object on a shelf.

"Whatever you think. It's not that important." Ben looked at the collection of office supplies he'd assembled. "I've got enough here. Let's close these boxes up again."

When his phone rang, he gave it a casual glance. Marcus Herrera. His gut clenched. Not again.

Chapter 23

Driving across the city, Ben coached himself. Answer the questions simply and truthfully, do not get ruffled, and if things get ugly remember the name of the attorney Sandy recommended.

He parked at the State Police building and walked inside, a casual and innocent man. Same interrogation room, same drill as Herrera walked in and greeted him. They took seats across from each other, the cop deftly guiding the process so Ben was facing a wall with a two-way mirror.

"We heard the two of you had a falling out," Marcus said, after the soft lead-in questions were done.

"You heard this from Raven's aunt? Or maybe her brother?"

The latter guess elicited a tiny reaction on Herrera's face.

Ben pressed on. "The Takannis are grieving, lashing out, looking for someone to blame." He slowed, keeping his voice level. "I feel for them. But it doesn't mean they're right."

"And what if they are?"

"You're taking the word of a family—an estranged family—over mine? Have you looked at my record? How many years I've counseled others? How many people I've helped?"

"I have," Herrera replied, even-toned and immovable.

"And do you know what we're dealing with here? With Zachary? Do you know what this is doing to him?" If Julie were here, she'd be giving this guy a piece of her mind, about how much Zac was struggling, and she would probably be ranting that he had no idea what families go through at times like this. If his lawyer were here, she'd tell him to keep his mouth shut, to only answer what he'd been asked.

Herrera gave him a hard look. "I know what they said *you've* done to the family, especially to Raven. Do you want to go there? The fact is, there's motive."

"You've got it wrong, Detective. As they do. I don't know what else to tell you, but you're investigating the wrong person."

Herrera shot him a look, ignoring everything Ben had said. "This argument on the night in question—it got heated. So, what happened? Was it about your son?"

"We've been through this," Ben replied. "Zac's lived with Raven most of his life, and we've managed visitation as seamlessly as we could. This time we were discussing the upcoming holidays and the fact that my wife and I live much closer now. There were words, but it was only … we were both tired at the end of a long day." He forced himself to pause; giving too much detail would trap him.

Marcus raised an eyebrow, his fingers steepled over the table as he let the silence stretch. "Understandable. Travel stress, long day, tempers flare."

Ben resisted the urge to fill in, counting on his composure to say more than words could. He'd been on the other side of this often enough to know the tactic.

"It wasn't the first time you argued, according to what we've been told," Marcus finally continued.

"We always worked it out," Ben insisted, maintaining eye contact. "When you're not living in the same place, parenting takes extra effort." He kept his tone even, refusing to rise to the bait.

"Worked it out by fighting in the parking lot of a hotel?" Marcus countered, leaning forward with an intensity that was designed to intimidate. "Hotel security camera shows some punching."

"No one threw any punches. It's simply not our style," Ben said, shifting back slightly. Although Raven had swung her bag at him. That's probably what the camera recorded.

"Voices got pretty loud," Marcus replied, flipping through his notes. "We've got someone saying they saw it all go down."

"Then someone is lying. There was nothing to see." The response came out more forcefully than Ben intended.

"Heard it all, saw a confrontation. But maybe they ducked inside the hotel, trying not to get involved."

So, someone heard their voices, didn't want to get involved, and now they *were* getting involved. That was pretty flimsy. Ben drew a deep breath, reining in his frustration, aware of Marcus's interest in his every movement. "I've got no reason to do anything like this. None."

Marcus remained unfazed, reviewing his papers with the detachment of a judge handing down a sentence. "Maybe not a *good* reason," he said without looking up. "But in my experience, it doesn't take one."

Ben struggled against a wave of distrust. Had Raven set him up, knowing his commitment, his need to be involved with Zac? No, she was angry, but not vindictive. He couldn't lose himself in conspiracies. This needed his focus, nothing else.

Marcus's expression suggested the same answer.

"Your son is here in town," Marcus repeated, like the detail was something Ben had been trying to hide. "We'd like to talk with him."

"Zac wasn't present during the argument. His mother and I have always been conscious of presenting a united front." He was a psychologist who specialized in this. His own marriage survived—and he and Julie thrived—despite these complex ties.

Marcus switched subjects. "The brake line was tampered with, a tiny hole punctured so some miles would go by before it completely failed," Marcus said bluntly, letting the implication dangle. "Someone wanted that car to go off the road."

"That's what we were told." Ben clenched his fists beneath the table. "I had nothing to do with it. When it became apparent my discussion with Raven was going nowhere, we agreed to table it for another day, I went back to the room where I joined my wife and slept all night."

Marcus leaned back, his pen resting idly on the paper. He seemed almost curious, as if intrigued by how Ben would navigate this minefield. "You're saying that you never left your wife's side?"

"That's exactly what I'm saying," Ben watched as Marcus jotted down his words. "Someone's lying," he repeated. "And if I had anything to hide, you think I'd say that?"

"The next morning—from the beginning," Marcus said, another switch of topic.

"We left for Tewa," Ben began, keeping his voice a steady shield. "Zac wanted to ride with Julie and me, so we three were in one car, Raven and Nathan in hers. Raven was following, since she didn't know the way."

Marcus wrote down his responses, forehead wrinkled. "How long was Ms. Takanni's car in the parking lot unobserved?"

"You're asking when the brake lines got cut? I have no idea. Sometime during the night or early morning hours. Where's your infallible security camera during that time?"

Herrera's stare was deliberate, meant to unnerve him. Ben almost regretted his flippant response. But not quite. He hoped to push Marcus to look elsewhere.

"So, Zac was with you," Marcus summarized, tapping his pen against the notepad. "Why did you change the plan?"

"Because having teenagers means changing plans," Ben replied, unable to keep the trace of irony from his voice. "Because Raven was in a mood. Because Zac wanted her to come with us to the pueblo. I thought if she saw him settle in, she'd be happier about leaving him with us for the rest of the visit."

"It's a long trip, driving all the way here from northern Washington state," Marcus commented. "Curious why she didn't just put the boys on a plane to meet you here." It wasn't a question, and Ben wasn't sure what type of response was expected.

Ben studied the detective, watching as Marcus's pen drew circles around some of his notes on the page. He had played this game before but always on a different field, one where patients held the stories and he helped them untangle the knots. Now he was on the other side, a psychologist in a therapy session where every statement felt dangerous, even to him.

A uniformed officer tapped on the door, came in at Herrera's request, and whispered something in his ear.

"Excuse me," Marcus said, standing abruptly and carrying the folder with him.

Was it Ben's imagination or did he have the look of someone who'd been called into the boss's office, and not for a fun chat?

It was fifteen full minutes before Herrera returned and Ben could immediately tell the tables had turned. The detective shot a couple more questions at him, pertaining to the damage to Raven's brakes. The tone was immediately adversarial.

"Do I need a lawyer?" Ben asked, edgy about the intense grilling.

"It's your right."

"Thank you. I am now exercising that right." He started to pull his phone out, but Marcus had signaled to someone on the other side of the two-way mirror and two more officers stepped into the room.

"Benson Pecos, you are under arrest for the murder of Raven Takanni and Nathan Yazzie Pecos."

Chapter 24

Hours dragged by. At least it felt like hours, maybe days. Booking, fingerprints, mug shot. Ben had never felt so humiliated in his life. He was being led to a cell when a female officer stopped his captor and said the suspect's attorney was present. The one with a hand on his elbow diverted him to a side room.

His two-minute phone call to Marguerite Lopez-Ortiz had finally brought the woman who would be defending his life. He'd been settled into a chair, cuffed to a ring in the center of the metal table. Again, that sense of mortification as the lock clicked, confining him.

"Ben? Hi, I'm Marguerite."

The woman who stepped into the room was in her mid-forties, with lustrous dark hair to her shoulders, tan slacks and a blue button-down shirt, with a classic navy blazer. Her watchband was silver and turquoise, as were the pair of elegant studs in her ears. She moved gracefully toward him and took the seat opposite.

"It's nice that Sandy Black gave me a heads-up that you might be calling. My secretary knew to let you right through."

Ben nodded and thanked her.

"By way of introduction, and so you know who you're dealing with, I'm a fifth-generation New Mexican whose grandmother was a civil rights activist. Graduated from UNM Law School, spent six years as a public defender before establishing my own practice specializing in criminal defense, with an emphasis on cases involving tribal jurisdiction. I've defended cases in both state and tribal courts and know the cultural protocols." She pulled a pair of reading glasses from her woven leather purse and got a legal pad and pen from her briefcase. "I know you're a doctor, a psychologist with a stellar reputation—yes, I Googled you. What I don't know is why you're here. Fill me in."

And so he did, relating the interviews nearly verbatim between himself and Detective Herrera.

"Is he alleging that you damaged the brake line yourself?" She gave a skeptical look.

"I'm not sure what he's alleging. He hinted at that but then moved on to other questions. The mood took a swift downturn after he was called out of the interview for a few minutes and returned, ready to throw me in the slammer."

The mild humor drew a smile. "Well, we aren't going to let you stay here long. I think I can get your arraignment hearing a bit of priority, and hopefully we'll have you out on bond in time to be home for dinner."

Relief flooded through him.

"I'll learn more later, during discovery, when we'll have access to all their evidence, but it seems today's new development was that they've recovered Ms. Takanni's phone and have been able to track her most recent calls." She pushed a handwritten list across the table to him. "Know any of these?"

He told her he recognized the Alaska area code for three of the numbers, and the boarding school the boys attended in Bellingham for a couple others. "I don't know the individual numbers offhand, but my wife might. She's been doing some investigating into what was going on in Raven's life prior to this trip."

"Is your wife law enforcement? Private investigator?"

"Nosy investigative reporter."

Marguerite laughed at that. "We'll get along great, I'm sure."

She stood, gathering her notes and pushing her reading glasses to the top of her head. "Let me make some calls. I know the judge." She gave him a conspiratorial wink. "Don't go anywhere."

* * *

When things began to move, they moved quickly. He was driven downtown and escorted to a courtroom, where Marguerite stood in the hallway, chatting with Sandy Black. Ben didn't get the chance to exchange words—his police guardian never let go—but soon they were seated at the defense table and a judge was asking how he pled to the charges. Not guilty was an easy answer.

Marguerite politely requested he be released on his own recognizance, to which the prosecutor said no way because of his having come from out of state. Fine, his lawyer stipulated, saying that Dr. Pecos and his wife had recently established residency here. She recited a list of reasons he was an upstanding citizen, including his education and his prestige job with IHS. She got the judge's agreement to a reasonable bail amount and her guarantee that he wouldn't leave the state.

Sandy stepped forward to post that personally, and Ben was free to walk out. They agreed to meet within a few days, once Marguerite and her team had a chance to review the case and do some investigating of their own.

She reached out and squeezed his hand. "Don't worry. We've got your back."

Sandy hung back and the two men walked out of the courthouse together. "I'll give you a ride back to your vehicle. I talked to Julie and suggested she stay at the apartment with Zac. She didn't think he needed to witness all this," Sandy told him as Ben gathered his personal possessions, strapped his watch to his wrist and stuck his wallet and phone in different pockets.

Ben had forgotten about his truck. It must have been sitting in the lot at the state police station the better part of the day, if the clock on Sandy's dashboard was accurate.

"Ben, there is something …" Sandy said as he started his car.

"Uh-oh, sounds ominous."

"Not terribly so. It's just that the board has decided it's best if you don't begin your new job until this thing is solved."

"You mean, until my name is cleared and I'm officially not a murderer."

"Ben, don't. No one believes that. Not about you."

Ben stared out the side window, watching the downtown buildings give way to wide boulevards filled with rush-hour traffic.

"Ben, listen to me. No one on this planet thinks you're a guy who could kill anyone."

"Herrera."

"Okay, there's *one* person, and he's only sticking with that story because it's his job."

But Ben could think of one or two more. He'd remembered one of those Alaska phone numbers from Marguerite's list.

Chapter 25

He'd been home less than fifteen minutes—just long enough to reassure Julie and caution her about not saying anything to Zac until the time was right—when the expected knock came at the door.

Rynah had told him (warned!) that as matriarch of the Takanni family she wanted to come to Albuquerque and escort her niece's body back to Alaska, where they would observe the proper rites of the Haida. Ben had futilely hoped she and E.J. would simply meet with someone from the medical investigator's office, perhaps even at the airport, and turn around to leave. But he'd received a text to the contrary. We should talk. Where are you living?

Ben had given the address of the apartment, on the theory that privacy would work better than a public place for this sort of thing.

The second knock was firmer, more emotional.

Ben filled his lungs, searching for the calm he needed, and opened the door to meet it head-on. Raven's brother stormed in, eyes blazing, while Rynah followed, her sorrow evident on her face and in her body posture.

E.J. stepped closer, his presence confrontational. "She's gone, Ben. Because of you!" The words hissed out through clenched teeth. His hands fisted at his sides, tension knotting his shoulders. Ben stepped in front of Julie, protective, edging away from the angry man in front of him.

"You're wrong," Ben said, his voice quiet but firm, trying to mask the tremor beneath it. "I didn't have anything to do with it."

Rynah, at least, had thoughts for her great-nephew. "E.J., keep your voice down. Where's Zac?"

Julie piped up. "In his bedroom, probably with earbuds on, but yes, please be cautious about what you say."

E.J.'s anger wasn't done. "You think you can say that and walk away clean? We know about the fight, about your argument with her!" A vein throbbed at his temple.

Ben's exhaustion from the trying day threatened to overwhelm him. He had expected anger, but the force of E.J.'s attack caught him off balance. They'd been friends, roommates at one point during their college years. He swallowed hard, trying to keep his composure, even though he suspected E.J. of being the one who embellished the details of his argument with Raven.

Rynah's hand touched E.J.'s arm with gentle authority. "This isn't helping," she said. "Raven would want us to know what caused the accident." Her words hung in the air, leaving room for reason amid the chaos.

Ben could see her raw grief, but at least it seemed she wanted to understand the truth.

E.J. pulled back slightly, the initial heat of his anger tempered but still smoldering. "I want to know what happened," he said, his voice thick. "Why did she die, Ben? Because you wanted to get her out of the way?"

Ben's instincts screamed at him to push back, to defend himself with equal intensity, but he reined himself in. Right now, being defensive was a futile path. He had to find a way to make them see beyond their grief and anger, to reach the place where healing could begin.

"It was never like that," Ben said, hearing the weariness in his own voice. "We argued, yes, but it was about scheduling holiday time for the boys. Not about me wanting to hurt her. Do you believe I could do that to her?"

The vulnerability in his words was all he had to offer, the only shield against the onslaught of blame. Rynah watched him closely, measuring his sincerity.

E.J. turned away, his shoulders tense, but Ben sensed a fracture there, a momentary break in the armor of his anger. It wasn't enough to heal the rift, but it was a beginning, a space where they might find common ground.

Rynah's gaze softened, her own struggles visible as she sought the best way forward. "I believe," she said slowly, "that there may be more to this than any of us understand right now. Let us take a moment to breathe, to find out if there's something none of us are seeing yet."

Her words created a silence that stretched across the room, a heavy quietness. Ben used that silence to steady himself, to find his footing, knowing he had to convince them that Raven may have had enemies that none of them had considered.

Rynah's eyes narrowed, not in suspicion but in thought. He watched as her expression shifted, the lines of sorrow deepening with the possibility that his words were true. She was considering it, and the relief of not being dismissed outright touched him.

"Explain," she said.

Ben drew in a shaky breath, focusing on the details he had pieced together. "I don't know everything, but I know it was supposed to look like an accident. Julie has been investigating, tracking leads."

Julie stepped forward, confident. Ben imagined her in the newsroom, a complete professional. She sketched out the various options, without naming names, as that could have set off a whole chain of retribution no one was ready for.

"It sounds like a lot of guessing, Ben. How do we know you're not covering your tracks," E.J. said, his skepticism still evident, but at least the accusation lacked the fire it once had.

"Julie's ideas are something we need to consider," Rynah countered. Her words were moderate but firm. She turned to Ben, meeting his eyes directly. "You're sure of this?"

"As sure as I can be. I want to find out who did this as much as you do."

E.J.'s face held conflicting emotions, but Ben saw the anger slowly recede, giving way to a cautious willingness to cooperate.

"We'll work together, then," Rynah said, the voice of the matriarch setting the tone.

"Don't think you're off the hook," E.J. said, but the edge in his voice had dulled.

If only you knew, Ben thought. At least, as a family, they'd covered some important ground. To his left, the click of a door opening caught everyone's attention. Zac stepped out of his bedroom, his features fuzzy with sleep.

"Auntie Rynah, you're here!" He loped across the room, the tall lanky teen ready for a warm hug from his soft, pillowy great-aunt.

Rynah's gaze met Ben's, her expression saying, *look what you did to this boy.*

And despite his best hopes, Ben knew the war wasn't yet over.

Chapter 26

A fresh haircut could make all the difference in the way a girl saw her day, Julie decided, looking in the mirror. Taking off a couple inches to get rid of split ends, freshening up the layers of curls … her head felt lighter, and with it her whole being.

The past week had brought nightmare upon nightmare—from Raven's accident to Zac's grief-filled mood swings to Ben's arrest. Through it all Julie had pitched in, trying to dig out the truth, to figure out answers. And now she'd decided to take one morning for herself.

Hair appointment first, mall trip second. She would need a winter coat, and the pre-holiday sales ads were showing up. She paid the stylist, adding a decent tip, and walked out into another seventy-degree day with that New Mexico sky that defied description.

Her hybrid car waited in the parking lot and she took a minute to sit in it and check her messages. Throughout the hair appointment her phone kept pinging with texts from numbers she recognized as colleagues. Now she saw that the notes were loaded with congratulations. She couldn't believe her story had blown up quite so huge, getting picked up by the major wire services and showing up as far away as London, Buenos Aires, and Paris.

Julie's mind swirled back to the Florida senator's smug face, and his tangled connections to organized crime.

The investigation had started like any other—a tip from a trusted source, something that seemed insignificant until she began peeling back layers. Senator Russell Landry, a polished charmer, had ties to drug cartels, a fact he concealed with enough false fronts and alibis to fill his expansive beach house. Julie recalled him at one of his swanky fundraisers that she'd attended, smiling and confident in his ability to control the story. His bluster had withered when she confronted him with proof. The thought brought her some satisfaction but also mild trepidation. Men like him didn't roll over quietly. But her editor had backed her a hundred percent, and now the story was headline news everywhere.

She started the car and drove toward Coronado Center, which she recalled as the largest mall in the city. Before she'd gone a mile, her phone rang. With a quick glance at the screen, she tapped the hands-free connection.

"Marie! It's been too long. I was planning to call you once we got settled here. What's up with you?"

"Hey, Jules. I think the major news is what's up with you, girl. A local story turned national. I'm jealous. Okay, no, I'm super happy for you. How does it feel?"

"Kind of strange, since I'm clear across the country

now. But still … lots of people sending congrats and all that."

"You're not getting any blowback are you?" Marie's voice changed tone, became quieter. "I mean, well, politicians don't always play nice."

"If you mean nastygrams from his office aides, nah."

"Oh, that's a relief. From what they're saying on the news, he's bluffing his way through, denying everything imaginable, portraying this as a smear campaign. Jake Flowers is in full damage-control mode, deflecting everything back on you."

"Because that's what they do, people in his position, right?" Julie pictured the thick file she'd started, where she documented everything on this guy. "And that's why I kept both electronic and hard copies of everything."

"Good for you." A phone rang in the background and Marie apologized for needing to end the call.

It was fine. Julie had reached the mall and managed to snag a parking spot near Macy's. She would find the perfect coat, treat herself to lunch, and hope the Takanni bunch had left town by the time she got home. Yes, a girl's day out was exactly what she needed.

Chapter 27

Ben stood in the living room, his heart unraveling as Zac packed his belongings, his defiance stark as he zipped the huge suitcase shut. Ben felt pierced to the core.

He took a deep breath, willing himself to maintain composure, to put his professional knowledge to work here. He kept his voice gentle. "Zac, I do understand about going with your uncle and great-aunt for the funeral potlatch, the ceremonies, but I thought you'd be back. Don't you feel that you and I belong together?" God, that sounded needy.

Zac held his gaze, unmoved. "I need to be with Mom's family in Alaska," he said, his words steady. "They understand me. It's where I belong."

The words landed like heavy stones. He could see Zac's maturity and resilience, but his next words cut deep.

"Alaska is where my roots are, not here. I don't like it here. I didn't like it much in Bellingham either. I need my real family now."

The sound of a key in the lock, pulled both their attention. Julie walked in, a shopping bag in one hand, dropping her keys into her purse with the other. Something was different about her hair was Ben's incongruous thought. The smile on her face instantly faded when she looked at him.

"What's wrong?"

He nodded toward Zac and the two large suitcases beside him.

"Zac? Honey, what's the matter?"

He explained it tersely. This wasn't a quick trip for a funeral, it was a permanent move.

"But you'll come back and spend time with us, too, right?" Julie did seem to genuinely want that.

"We'll see. Maybe."

A tap at the door caught Ben's attention. When Rynah and E.J. entered, they positioned themselves firmly by Zac's side. In full-on lawyer mode, Rynah's presence was commanding, her gaze sharp as she assessed Ben. The realization hit: they'd been conversing privately with Zac, making their case for this move.

"Family is everything, Benson," Rynah said, her voice a firm edict. "Zachary's lineage passes through the mother's. He is Haida—Kaigani. Our tribe is where he needs to be."

Ben felt her words tearing at him as he recognized their truth. Most Native cultures held to the same matriarchal system of belief. He struggled with knowing that this was something more than his own desires.

E.J. stepped forward, his posture challenging. "You

can't just come and go in his life," he said, his voice clipped. "This moving around is upsetting to his interactive spiritual energy, his connection with the natural world. Zac belongs with us, with those who knew Raven."

Ben looked at Zac, trying to bridge the chasm growing between them. "Zac, I want to be there for you. I love you. That hasn't changed."

Zac's expression flickered with emotion, a struggle playing out within him. Ben could see his son caught between love for his father and the pull of his mother's family. He knew the devastation of parental bickering over children, and he couldn't become a part of that.

"You're important to me," Zac said, his voice wavering. "But Mom's family—they need me too."

Although Ben felt hollow at this moment, he understood the cultural and familial significance of Zac's choice. Raven's body was being taken back to Alaska, and with it Zac's desire to be with those who shared her blood and memory.

The situation was slipping beyond his grasp, but this was something he could not force. "I understand," Ben said finally, though it felt like a feeble admission. "But I'm here for you, Zac. I'm always here."

He turned to Julie, searching for support. Her eyes met his, empathetic and compassionate. "This is between you and Zac," she said softly, but Ben sensed more unspoken beneath her words. Something uneasy gnawed at him, something he couldn't quite name.

Rynah's voice broke the tension. "You can come visit him in Alaska," she said, extending a thread of hope. "Be part of his life there."

Visit. Ben nodded, clutching at the offer, though the

words felt tenuous and his eyes prickled. Visiting was all he'd ever achieved with his son, never a permanent home together.

He watched as Zac and the Takannis turned to leave, E.J. taking the handle of the larger suitcase. Rynah's final look was firm but not unkind, a reminder of where Zac belonged. As the door closed behind them, the silence returned. It reminded him of other times when Zac, then both of the boys, would leave him to live with Raven. But this was different. The whole atmosphere of the room carried unfamiliar emotions.

Intellectually, Ben knew it was something they'd have to navigate, one unsteady step at a time. Physically, it felt as if a part of him had shattered.

The positive side of it was that Zac would not be here to witness his father standing trial for murder. When Julie reached for his hand, Ben knew she was thinking the same thing.

Chapter 28

Julie hung her new winter coat in the bedroom closet, her morning of shopping and having her hair done now seeming stupidly frivolous in light of everything else. When she walked back to the living room, she spotted Ben in the kitchen fiddling with the coffee maker.

"Hey. You doing okay?"

"As well as you would imagine." He took a mug from the cupboard and raised an eyebrow to see if she wanted one. "The ironic thing is that I counsel people all the time on this kind of thing. I'm either talking to the rebellious teens who want to leave home or to parents who've become lonely empty nesters. Nothing about those talks prepared me for having it happen to me. I can't believe I'd begun to see all their stories as repetitious, same thing every time. It doesn't feel that way now."

"Oh, honey." She pulled him close and wrapped her arms around his middle. When she stood back and studied his face, all the worry and stress of recent days was clearly evident there. "Listen. For one thing, your story is different. Well, everyone's is, but your kid lost his mother to a murderer. And the two of you haven't exactly had the typical father-son relationship. Ever. From the beginning."

He winced but nodded.

"So do not beat yourself up over not knowing exactly what to do, how to deal with it. It's going to take time."

"And that's exactly what I would be saying to a patient or their family."

"Think I should become your partner in your counseling job?" Her quirky smile told him she was merely trying to lighten the mood.

He reached over and wound one of her curls around his finger. "You did something new here, didn't you? And what else besides this and a new coat? Did you have a nice morning on your own?"

"It was fun, pampering myself a bit." She remembered Marie's phone call and the comments about the senator's aides. Some tiny memory lingered but Ben's phone ringing interrupted that thought.

"Hmm, it's my lawyer. Never thought I'd need one of those." His mouth twisted but he picked up the call and put it on speaker.

"Can we do a meeting this afternoon, four o'clock, my office?" It came out sounding more like a command appearance than a request. "I've got some new information and I'd like for you to meet someone."

Ben and Julie exchanged a glance as he ended the call. Ben offered a comforting smile and she handed him the coffee mug. "We'll handle it together. Like we always do." His voice was steady, but Julie could see the concern. "Zac's move to Alaska. You were relieved."

"I was," she admitted. "Right now, it feels like the safest place he could be."

"Maybe we'll head up there when this is over," Ben suggested, only half-teasing.

* * *

Marguerite Ortiz's office was downtown in a converted bungalow an easy two-block walk from the courthouse. Julie supposed that was by design, exactly the right location for a defense attorney. And although the tan stucco exterior of the flat-roofed building was unimpressive—no high-rise office of glass and steel for this lady—it spoke of humble beginnings and not wasting money on fancy digs or a huge staff.

A receptionist greeted them by name and offered beverages, which they both declined. Marguerite emerged from an inner office and waved them through. Julie introduced herself, immediately impressed by the lawyer's quiet confidence and casual attire. The offices had obviously once been a home, with the original living room now the reception area and lobby. One of the former bedrooms was Marguerite's office, the other a conference room. They walked into the latter.

"I'd like you to meet the private investigator I'm working with on your case. Ron Parker, meet Ben and Julie Pecos."

Parker, a man in his mid-forties with sharp eyes and thinning brown hair, stepped forward. His professional demeanor came through, even in jeans and a plaid shirt. Julie noticed a slight limp as he moved toward them. She sensed there was a story behind that. She also sensed that he was sizing them up, based on something he already knew.

Marguerite walked to one end of the conference table, where she'd left a file folder, and the others took seats. "RJP Investigations is terrific, and Ron is the best PI in the city for this type of case, as well as being a whiz at background checks and digging through internet archives. And you still work with …?"

"My younger sister is a partner. Charlie is … well, she's quite a pistol, persists until she catches the bad guy." With a wink toward Julie, he added, "You'd like her."

"Ron has lots of connections, gets answers in a hurry. And, if I may say it … both he and Charlie are not afraid to get their hands dirty." Marguerite sent a smile toward the investigator.

She opened the file and flipped a few pages. "What we've got since yesterday—the police recovered Ms. Takanni's phone and are having their forensic lab go through it. They claim there's not enough info to share yet, but I did manage to get a list of the numbers in her recent calls. Ben, you saw some of those yesterday. Now, Ron has cross-referenced those so we have names to match them." She pulled two printed pages from the folder and slid them across the table to Ben.

Julie leaned in to look at it. "I recognize several of these." She went on to explain the gist of her online research and how she came up with potential enemies, both within the sled dog racer community and from Raven's aggressive business competitor.

"Can you forward those materials to me?" Ron asked.

"Happily. Our theory has been, since the police said the brake line was intentionally tampered with, that Raven had enemies. Once their entire case focused on Ben, we knew we needed to learn more about what was going on in her life back home."

"Plus, from the moment we met up, here in Albuquerque, Raven's mood was decidedly sour. She'd usually been cooperative with us when it came to making arrangements for the boys, and this time she was like a surly old bear. Something was going on, and we suspect it started way before this road trip." Ben kept his voice level, but Julie could hear the tension under the surface.

Marguerite lowered her glasses and met their gaze. "We've got some great leads here, and RJP has my authorization to travel north, to follow-up and question these people, if necessary," she said, her tone exuding control.

Julie glanced at Ben. His expression reflected hope.

Ron cleared his throat. "We will follow up the leads, starting wherever you left off, Julie. If it appears one of these parties, either in Washington or Alaska, is involved we'll discover it and we can arrange to have them officially questioned."

Having someone on their team, especially these two who gave great take-charge vibes, made it feel as if a huge weight had been lifted. Julie could tell by Ben's demeanor that he felt it too.

"Okay, I want you two to get some sleep," Marguerite said, pushing her chair back from the table. "It's pretty obvious that you've been through hell. We'll need you rested and relaxed when we begin taking depositions."

Ben's phone had vibrated with an incoming message, which he'd ignored. He glanced now at his screen. "Vicente," he whispered under his breath. "Marguerite, I have one question. I may need to make a trip—hopefully a quick one—up to Tewa in the next day or two. Will that be a problem?"

"You're asking because the judge warned you not to leave."

He nodded.

"Don't leave New Mexico," she said. "And I'd add a caution that wandering very far could raise some eyebrows. But an hour away, to visit family, I don't think that's a problem." She sent him a quick smile. "Just be sure you come back."

It was nearly six o'clock when they walked out of the attorney's office. Her receptionist had gone for the day, and Ron Parker walked out with them.

"Here's my business card," he told Julie. "Whatever leads you've gathered, if you can email them to me that would be great. And if we need to meet in person, let me know and we'll set up something."

They watched him walk over to a red Mustang convertible before they got into Julie's car.

Ben pulled out his phone to return Vicente's call. He listened, expression grave. "Thanks for sharing that, man. Let me ask you, do you feel like harming yourself or anyone else?"

A short reply, which Julie couldn't hear.

"That's good. Now listen for a second. If you do start to feel that way, I want you to call 911, get to the hospital, and tell them what you've told me. I mean it. If you think you'll be okay for a while longer, I'll drive up in the morning. First thing, I promise."

Whatever his cousin said, it must have reassured Ben. He ended the call and dropped the phone into the cup holder between them.

"Sounds kind of serious. A 911 call?"

Ben shook his head. "I had to ask that question. It's required. I got the distinct impression he's high right now and talking smack about all kinds of things. From what Aunt Dora told me, he does this at least a couple times a month."

"Oh dear."

"Yeah. It's worrisome, and I do need to help him. But, with Zac leaving and everything else, this day has been way too emotional for me to be of much use to anyone else. Marguerite was right. I need rest, decent sleep. And Vicente needs to come down off whatever he's taken before I'll be able to get through to him anyway." He sighed. "If I can't report to my new job and help other people, at least I hope I can help my troubled cousin."

She reached across the console and took his hand. "You're such a good man, Ben Pecos."

Chapter 29

Ben parked and sat for a moment, breathing in the scents of autumn and woodsmoke—his favorite memories of the pueblo. Leaving Albuquerque this morning, he'd driven beneath and beside a wonderland of colorful globes at the northern edge of the city. He thought it was the final day of the Balloon Fiesta, but he wasn't sure. At any rate, the brilliant colors and carefree look of them was enough to brighten his mood.

Now, at Tewa, the adobe structures clustered like ancient guardians, and the mountains in the background marked the horizon. He parked in front of his aunt's house and stepped out of the truck. Before he had closed the door, Aunt Dora swept him into a hug that smelled of warmth and earthy oven bread. "How was the drive?" she asked, her voice rising over the sounds of kids playing somewhere nearby.

"It's getting somewhat easier with every trip." Ben smiled, taking in her familiar face, the comfortable disorder of the woodpile on the porch, three pairs of work boots lying where their owners had stepped out of them, and a discarded red ballcap. Neither of them brought up the recent tragedy.

She released him, wrapping her shawl more closely around her shoulders, patting his arm as if making sure he was actually there. "We're glad you made it. Come in, it's warmer in the house."

He paused and touched her arm. "Dora, tell me, how's Vicente this morning?"

"Himself." She stared at the ground for a moment. "Really, he's doing all right."

He followed her inside, and the cold gave way to the comfort of the warm adobe home and welcoming voices. He stepped over to the crackling fire in the corner fireplace and held out his chilly hands.

"We've got some breakfast left, eggs and toast, if you're hungry."

"I ate before I came, thanks."

"Okay, that's fine. I want to get the stew on to simmer for tonight's dinner. It's kind of crazy in here right now."

The distinct scent of red chile filled the air. He followed Dora into the kitchen, which was alive with laughter and the clatter of dishes, the central table crowded with family and the chaos of food preparation. Aunt Zena kneaded dough with powerful, steady hands. A younger cousin perched on a chair, cutting meat into chunks as she giggled at something one of the aunts had said. Ben's entrance prompted a chorus of greetings, and someone rushed to clear a space at the table.

He leaned over to look at the lean meat pieces. "Venison?"

"Elk," she replied. "Elroy and Herman got a nice one this year."

"Sit, sit," said a voice over the din. "You can rest before we put you to work."

Ben grinned, shaking his head. "I'll rest later. Let me help."

His aunt directed him to a stack of onions waiting for attention. Of course she did—chopping the onion was the job Julie always gave him, too.

He slipped off his jacket, rolled up his sleeves, and took up a knife, at ease in the midst of the bustling activity. Happy to fit in. Someone removed the red chiles from the oven and put them in water to soak, while another measured oregano, cumin, and cornmeal. Soon, he was part of the conversation that darted around the room.

While Dora acted as head chef, calling for ingredients as she needed them, Vicente walked in, glassy eyed, a coffee mug in hand. He grunted a hello. Ben started to set down his knife, ready to talk if the time was right. But his cousin set the mug on the sideboard and slumped out the back door. After yesterday's call when his cousin had been excitable and almost talking gibberish, this was clearly the crash after the dopamine high.

"Ben! Look at this!" One of the younger kids pulled his attention away. He would need to catch up with Vicente later. Until the mood leveled out, Ben probably wouldn't get far with a conversation.

Ben handed over his pile of chopped onion and stepped to the sink to wash the scent off his hands. The stew would take some hours of simmering to become *fat,* thick enough for the cornbread and oven bread to dip into it. He wandered outside. Maybe Vicente would want to talk, but he didn't see his cousin right away. Strolling past the post office and the spot where he'd previously seen the packet change hands, he saw none of that group either.

Elmore Waquie's police cruiser came rolling along the dirt road, stopping in front of the post office. "Ben Pecos," he greeted as he got out.

The old cop was heavier and grayer than Ben remembered, and the lines around his mouth drooped more, but he was still the same man who'd been police chief of the pueblo as long as Ben could remember.

"Hello, Elmore."

"How are you, Ben? I heard about the accident. What's it been, a couple weeks ago now? So sorry."

Eight days, actually. Ben nodded and thanked him. He was getting used to deflecting condolences rather than letting the words pierce his gut the way they did during the first few days. He stood still, wondering whether the police grapevine included the fact that he'd been arrested.

Apparently not. Elmore wished him well and walked inside the post office. Ben headed in the other direction, hoping to spot Vicente, but not wanting to get into other conversations, especially about the accident. He covered nearly all the streets, beginning in the center of the pueblo, meandering really, until his gut and his smart watch told him the chile stew was likely ready. He realized the sun was low in the sky. Where had the hours gone?

Back at Dora's house, people edged in from other rooms, drawn by the scents and the promise of food. Ben's aunt circled the room as people filled bowls with the savory stew. She set a gentle hand on Ben's arm and directed him to the stove to do the same. He felt the threads of his family and heritage tighten around him, a comforting web of belonging.

Ben found himself next to his uncle at the table. He spotted Vicente across the room and was glad to see him back with the group, and eating. He didn't see any sign that his cousin was high again. Maybe they actually would get to have a reasonable talk about the subject.

After fifteen or twenty minutes, Uncle Joe pushed his own empty bowl back and cleared his throat, commanding everyone's attention. Instinctively, they knew it was story time.

"These are stories my grandfather told," his uncle said, passing on more than words. "They teach us who we are, and we must keep them alive."

Ben nodded, aware of the younger cousins who paused their chatter to listen. People quieted around him, lulled by the familiar narrative.

"You know the story of Agoyo P'in, who carried his medicine bag whenever he heard the cry of an animal in need of care. Did I ever tell you of the time Agoyo P'in saved one of our own baby goats with a feather?"

Uncle Joe paused to let that remarkable statement sink in. "He came into the pen and his gentle touch told him what the baby goat needed. From his medicine bag, Agoyo P'in pulled a feather, which he cut with his sharp knife." With hand motions, Joe demonstrated.

"He made the shaft of the feather into a straw with a sharp point. Then he inserted the point into the goat's throat. No blood came out. And Agoyo P'in gently blew into the straw, so the baby goat could breathe easily again." Bestowing a smile, Joe looked around at the group. "He told me the goat was fond of cactus and I must keep it away from that. So I did. And that baby goat grew up to be mother of the strongest goats in the herd."

His uncle let the last words of the story settle like dust motes in the light, and Ben felt a quiet satisfaction that resonated deeper than he'd expected. Joe looked directly at Ben, even as the others chatted together about what a miracle that the goat could be saved with a feather. Ben wondered, was this a metaphor for his role with Vicente? The cure might sting, could possibly draw blood, but in the end the patient would be stronger and could go on to do great things. He smiled back at his uncle. Message received.

He thought of his life away from this place, of the people he'd tried to help as a psychologist and how these stories informed that work. Every time he returned, he found new insights in the old words. It was a kind of learning that stretched beyond any college degree, a deep and intuitive understanding that came from belonging.

Later, he excused himself from the table, leaving the hum of voices behind. He stepped out to the covered porch, staring at the shadows of the pueblo in the moonlight. The evening had grown colder in the way that desert nights did. The buildings, the people, the stories—they were a constant in a world where he had often felt caught between places. The knowledge grounded him, allowing him to embrace both his roots and his path forward.

"Glad you're here, Benson," Vicente spoke from the doorway, and Ben smiled at the sound of his cousin's voice.

"Me too," he replied.

The night air was a sharp force, lit with stars and the distant call of coyotes, and Ben was glad he'd picked up his jacket before coming outside. Ben and Vicente walked into the road, leaving the family chatter behind like a comfortable sweater. The sky expanded above, endless, the birthplace of many stories. Ben leaned against a hitching post in front of a darkened house, staring at the moonlit outlines of rooftops.

Vicente's words broke the stillness. "You coming back like this," he said. "You make it seem easy."

Ben nodded. "It's not always. Sometimes I wonder where I belong."

His cousin hesitated, then spoke into the night. "You're not the only one."

Ben turned toward Vicente, recognizing something in his voice. "You feel that way too?"

Vicente kicked at a loose stone, the movement betraying his frustration. "Yeah, I do. Everyone expects me to stay here, to be the one who never leaves, you know? But sometimes, I feel like I don't fit here, or anywhere."

Ben listened, his skin tingling. He hadn't known his cousin struggled with these thoughts, the same ones that followed him to far-off cities. "It's hard, being caught between places. You're a part of everything and nothing at the same time."

"Exactly," Vicente looked at Ben, a curious mix of envy and empathy in his gaze. "You make it look easy. Going away, then coming back and picking up like you never left."

Ben shook his head. "It's never that simple. I always feel like I'm missing something, no matter where I am."

Silence wrapped around them like the night. The faint echo of laughter from inside reminded Ben of the warmth they'd left behind, and the distance he sometimes felt from it. "It's different for you," he said, measuring his words. "You've got deep roots here."

Vicente's voice turned bitter. "That's what everyone thinks. I don't know if I'm strong enough to live up to them."

"Maybe it's not all about being strong. What are your dreams, your vision for yourself?"

Vicente shrugged. "I don't know."

But Ben sensed more and waited quietly for him to formulate his next words. Ben's experience in the white man's world was that people felt a need to jump in and say something, anything, to offer advice right away. But here at the pueblo he remembered his grandfather's way, to simply wait, to give the person time.

"As a kid, I admired your mother's talent with pottery. Kind of wanted to do that myself."

"Really?" Surprise didn't quite cover it. Vicente, the bully with an artistic soul? "What style was your favorite?"

"I was in awe of her storytellers, the way she created the little kids' expressions as they listened to the elder." Vicente scuffed at the dirt with the toe of his sneaker. "I don't know. I have no training. Not sure I even have the skill."

Ben resisted offering advice, to tell his cousin he could surely find a mentor, suggesting he get some clay and experiment. They could get to that later.

"They pushed me to raise corn and tend goats. By the end of the day there's no energy to come home and make art, you know?"

Ben nodded. He knew about the pressures of tribal history and family, and how easily it could crush a person beneath its expectations. He felt the tension in Vicente's words, the doubts that seemed almost foreign coming from his confident cousin. He needed to address both the dreams Vicente felt he'd missed out on, but also the current and very real problems.

"What about the stuff you said to me last night, when you called?" Ben tried to read his cousin's expression in the moonlight.

"Drugs. I know. I'm a screwup. I see it on my mother's face all the time."

"She's worried. We're all worried, man." Ben stared up at the stars, waiting a few beats. "It would be cool if you figured out a way to replace that, to let art take the place of whatever it is the drugs are doing for you."

Vicente leaned back, the wooden porch creaking beneath him. "And how do I do that, move beyond addiction?"

Ben thought of his mother's struggles with alcohol. He took a breath, finding honesty in the chilly air. "We can start by admitting it's not easy. And maybe by working together, finding solutions that make sense."

A nod from Vicente, tentative but hopeful, showed Ben that his words had connected. "You think there's a place for me out there?"

Ben felt the yearning, the same one that pulled him away and brought him back. "There's a place for you, Vicente. As a sober person and as an artist. What you're going through isn't a personal failure. You're hurting and could use professional help."

He stepped back, raising both palms. "And I'm not saying that I'm the best source for that. Someone completely outside the family might be more appropriate to help you with an evaluation and a treatment plan."

Vicente nodded slowly, absorbing the ideas.

"I can recommend someone, there are good people with Indian Health Service, and I'm sure we could make it as convenient as possible for you." Ben stared again at that impossibly wide night sky, brilliant with stars. Venus shone above the mountain to the east. "Thank you for sharing, Vicente. That couldn't have been easy for you."

"Hey, cuz, you've had your own share."

It was Ben's turn to be amazed. His cousin had never shown much interest in Ben's very different journey. "It was harder for me as a kid, coming from a mixed family. The way Grandma wanted me to live, with Anglos, it made things … complicated."

Vicente's response was surprisingly thoughtful. "You always had one foot in each world. Guess I never thought how that might be. I just figured you were lucky."

"It's not luck," Ben replied. "It's what I learned to deal with."

They walked side by side, two silhouettes against the canvas of stars, and Ben felt their silent bond draw tighter. They were almost back to Dora's house now.

Vicente rubbed his bare arms against the evening chill, but his voice had lost its earlier edge. "When you talk like that, it makes me see things differently."

Ben looked at him, saw a brotherhood he hadn't expected, and felt gratitude for it. He'd been struggling for answers on his own, quite possibly the reason he'd gone into psychology as a profession. "Maybe this time we can figure it out together."

"Yeah." Vicente nodded. "Let's do that."

Ben sensed a shift, a realignment of everything he'd thought he knew about his cousin. A stubborn pride, a shared vulnerability, and the bravery to confront them both.

"You know," Vicente said, his tone lighter. "We have a chance to see if these solutions work."

"How?"

"We're doing a traditional ceremony tomorrow morning. Want to come?"

The prospect opened something inside Ben, a space he hadn't realized needed filling. "I'd like that."

Dora's front porch felt like a small, safe island. Ben and Vicente lingered there, content with the silence. Golden light from the window spilled onto the porch, mingling with starlight and moon shadows. Inside, Ben could hear the family quieting, the cousins having left for their own houses, the evening winding down into the softness of sleep.

He turned to Vicente. "You know, we're not the only ones. There are lots of people caught between places, like us."

Vicente nodded, his profile thoughtful. "Sometimes, I look at the old guys around here, the ones who have it all figured out, and I wonder if I'll ever get there."

"I think we both will," Ben replied. "But maybe it'll look different for our generation."

Vicente glanced over, the familiar cocky grin making a return. "You mean with you running off every other week? Yeah, it'll be different."

"I won't run off this time," Ben promised. He thought of his aunts and uncles, of how they filled the house with stories and food and the richness of tradition. "Let's stay out here a while longer. I'm not sleepy yet."

They stood on the porch, wrapped in the clarity of the New Mexico sky and the honest exchange of two lives intersecting. For the first time in years, Ben felt anchored to the ground beneath his feet.

Chapter 30

Ben's call had surprised her. Vicente was talking, really talking, to him for the first time Ben could ever remember. He'd decided to stay at Tewa overnight and attend a ceremony the next day. And although she felt a tiny speck of trepidation at the idea of her first night completely alone in the apartment, she reminded herself to put on her big-girl panties and be brave.

Plus, she had all those materials to assemble, make sense of, and send to Ron Parker the private investigator.

She sat at the dining table, once again thinking how nice it would be to have a dedicated home office once they got settled. The surface was littered with notes and pages she'd printed from the internet, and she'd begun to get them into a semblance of order, making stacks for different subjects.

Now, she needed to type up notes that the PI could

make sense of. The first email became so full and convoluted that she changed the subject line and divided the topics. Two hours later, she had three separate emails: Raven Takanni — activism; Raven Takanni — tattoo business; Raven Takanni — dogsledding and racing.

Within each message were links to the sites and social media pages Julie had discovered, documents she had saved, and miscellaneous tidbits that pertained. It felt strange, as a journalist, to be giving someone else her source materials. She still had her own copies, of course, but this was sharing on a level she'd never done before, even with her editors. She reminded herself that this was different. Ben's freedom, maybe his life, were on the line.

The last item she came to, before hitting Send on the three emails, was the mysterious note she'd found on her windshield, the one warning her to stop poking around. She snapped a photo of it, attached it to one of the messages, and told Parker about the circumstances. If he wanted to see the original, he was welcome. She hesitated to let it out of her possession but if it was related, he should have it.

When she'd offered it to Detective Herrera, he had pooh-poohed any possible connection, and then things had moved so fast, with Ben's arrest and needing to hire Marguerite. And now, here they were.

Less than thirty minutes later, her phone rang and she saw it was Ron, the PI.

"Julie, first, thanks. The info you sent looks great and I'll check it out." He cleared his throat. "Got a question about the note, the one you said was on your windshield. To be clear, this was here in Albuquerque and it came after you'd been doing all this research?"

"Yes, exactly. It was creepy because it seemed apt for

what I'd been working on. Yet, I don't see how any of the subjects of my searches could have known where to find me."

"Yeah, I agree. That's weird."

"I did have my car checked out by a mechanic and nothing had been messed with."

"Did you show the note to the police?"

"The detective at the state police office took a quick look and tossed it back. He was too busy making his case that Ben is a killer."

"Okay, you do have the original note still?"

"I do."

"I'd like to get that if you don't mind. A buddy from my police days still does me a favor from time to time, and I'll see if he can pull fingerprints from it. No guarantees. People have wised up and often wear gloves, but we'll see what we get."

"Sure, anytime. You can pick it up or I can meet you somewhere."

Papers rustled in the background. "Marguerite gave me your address … right off Academy and San Mateo? It's on my way home, if you don't mind my interrupting your dinner."

"Come on by." Unless a plate of cheese and apple slices was considered dinner, he wouldn't be interrupting anything.

"Twenty, twenty-five minutes." He ended the call without waiting for an answer.

Julie tidied the table surface, rearranging her stacks of paper but not putting it all away. Ron might want to look at some other random thing she'd saved. It felt like a relief to have help with this, to know there were professionals on her side.

She was flipping through the Netflix selections when a tap came at the door, startling her. She verified through the peephole that it was Ron Parker.

"Hi, thanks for stopping by," she said, letting him in and reaching for the plastic baggie with the note in it. "You saved me another drive downtown."

He flattened the bag and stared at the note. "It does appear to be actually handwritten. Some of the fonts people find for their printers can be pretty darn convincing."

"I thought about that too. It's why I bagged it right away. My prints will be on there."

"And hopefully those of only one other person. It would be nice if that person is in the system. We may not know for a few days, and I will report. Meanwhile, be sure to let me know if you think of anything else that could help." He spotted the boxes stacked in the corners. "Looks like you folks are in the process of getting settled."

They'd given him a quick rundown of their recent move and Ben's new job. "We're purchasing a house, an older one in the original country club neighborhood, but it's being renovated so we're looking at a few more weeks before we can move in."

He nodded. "Yep, those things take time." Then his gaze traveled to the shelf they'd set up for the TV and miscellaneous items. "That's cute—a souvenir of your Florida time?"

Julie's eyes followed where he was pointing. The carved wooden alligator.

"Oh gosh, I hadn't even thought about this." She went into the story of the two wrapped gifts they'd found among their possessions. "Ben and I thought maybe the neighbors tucked them in when they helped us pack, you know, a surprise going-away present. But I've called the ones I thought might have done it and no one has a clue."

"May I see it?"

She stepped over and picked it up. "There was a photo, too."

Ron was turning the carved piece over in his hands. "Interesting."

Meanwhile, she'd located the photo and showed it to him. "Weird gifts, huh? We never did figure out who took the picture."

"I'd say this was taken with a long telephoto lens. It shows in the less-than-sharp edges on the image."

Julie felt a chill run down her arms. "That's creepy. The kid is Ben's son and we were on an outing to the Everglades."

"I don't want to freak you out, Julie, but could I take these for further examination?" He said nothing more.

Chapter 31

The sun was still an imagined warmth, hidden beyond the horizon, when Ben woke to the importance of the day ahead. The house lay in the quiet throes of sleep. He slipped into the traditional clothes of his ancestors, each item a memory of his mother. Aunt Zena had saved these items for him, all these years, he realized.

His tribal lineage came through Nia Pecos; his Anglo heritage from his father didn't matter. A few years ago, he thought he'd found the man, but DNA proved that not to be true and Ben had moved on. Still, he now understood Zac's being drawn to Raven's clan, and Rynah's. These things were older than time, certainly beyond the whim or desire of any one person.

As he stepped into the deep blue of predawn, Vicente's figure emerged beside him, and they moved toward the ceremony grounds, unburdened by any need for words.

The village was alive but still. So still, so quiet, compared to the city. The first hint of dawn turned the sky from deep indigo to pale gray. Ben felt the soft fabric of his ceremonial clothing brush against his skin, a tactile reminder of why he was here. He touched the edge of his shirt, fingered the seams that held stories created by his grandmother. The morning felt pure, uncomplicated.

Vicente walked at his side, also dressed for the ceremony, and the simple fact of his presence was a comfort. It tethered Ben to the reality of the moment, a grounding influence that allowed his mind to wander without drifting too far. He looked at his cousin, the easy stride and familiar profile. It was new, this openness between them, since their conversation last night. He'd been concerned that Vicente might have forgotten about this morning's plan, or slipped. Or rejected their connection.

Ben saw movement ahead as other figures converged on the ceremony grounds—family, friends, the wider community. They gathered in quiet reverence, preparing for what was to come. Ben and Vicente joined the loose circle.

Ben watched as people settled into position, and he found his spot among the elders, humbled by their acceptance and their legacy. He settled, realizing his heartbeat matched the rhythm of the lone drum. Across the circle he met Vicente's gaze, a silent exchange that reinforced their conversation from the previous evening.

Songs began, blending with the drumbeat, telling the ancient stories in Tewa, the nearly extinct language that felt older than time. It was a language of connection, and yet fewer than two thousand people in the world today actually spoke it. And although Ben understood only a few of the words, he let it pull him in, closer to the center of himself.

Each gesture of the ceremony felt sacred in its simplicity. Ben followed the elders. He felt his strands of hesitation unravel, replaced by a sense of belonging that filled him completely. Here, in this circle, he knew who he was.

The ceremony concluded with a grace as profound as its beginning. The silence that followed was not an absence but a fullness, a lingering echo of the ritual. Ben stood still, letting the moment settle into him.

Around him, tribal members began to move, to speak in hushed tones, to gather their things. Ben remained for a while, alone with his thoughts, in no rush to leave, no pull to be elsewhere. This new certainty of his identity and purpose filled him with peace.

When he finally moved, it was with the knowledge that he carried something enduring. The early morning, the circle of voices, the gentle rise of smoke—they were part of him now, inseparable from his being. He turned toward the familiar figures of his aunts, uncles, and cousins, joining them with steps that felt light.

Ben knew there would be more to learn, more to understand, but the ceremony's power extended beyond its end, affecting him in ways he hadn't anticipated. Aunt Zena, his mother's sister, touched his arm in a gesture full of meaning, and he smiled at her in return. He knew what she saw in him, and he saw it too.

As the circle dispersed, Ben remained quietly at its center, absorbing the tradition that wrapped around him like a protective cloak. He welcomed it, embraced it, and let it guide him as the first rays of sunshine crawled over the mountain to illuminate the pueblo.

Ben walked back to his grandmother's former home as the morning sun stretched long shadows across familiar paths. Returning to the room where he'd slept, he changed into his regular clothing, hanging his ceremonial regalia in the closet, saving the precious items for the next time.

In the bustling kitchen, Aunt Zena caught him in a knowing smile, and together they stepped onto the porch. She held his gaze, her voice tranquil. "This is home, Benson," she said, pressing an eagle feather into his hand.

The feather's soft weight was more profound than Ben could express, a tangible link to his clan. He looked at his mother's youngest sister, seeing the wisdom in her face. "It is," he agreed. "Thank you for reminding me."

She touched his cheek, a gentle gesture. "Sometimes we forget what's right here in front of us. You need to hold on to it."

"I will," Ben promised. "There's a lot to hold on to."

She nodded, the lines of her face deepening with a smile. "And a lot to give back."

He watched his family through the window, their movements familiar as they prepared food for the day. He held the eagle feather carefully. "It's not easy, living in both worlds," he whispered.

"It's not supposed to be," Zena replied, although the words brought comfort rather than chastisement. "Having you here, seeing you participate with the community, that's how we make it through, by being there for each other."

"I'll find ways to do more," he said. "I promise."

"You're already doing it, Benson, helping your cousin, helping Indians from other tribes. We are so proud." She beamed at him with the same love he'd seen at the ceremony.

Ben felt the urgency of the road ahead, dreading what awaited him in Albuquerque. He wanted to carry this morning's sensations with him, to let it soothe his soul in the tough days and weeks ahead. He turned the feather in his hands, seeing it as more than a symbol. It was a guide.

"Thank you," he said again, the words encompassing more than he could explain.

Zena's gaze held him, grounding him. "Go, do what you need to do."

Ben left the porch, heading toward his truck. He spotted Vicente there, leaning against the driver's side door. Ben tossed his overnight bag in the back. "Hey, man. I'm glad you waited here."

They did a quick fist-bump. "I don't know how to thank you, Ben."

"I'm happy to see that you want to make a change. You're still the one who has to do the work. I'll send you a referral to another counselor. It's usually better for family members to have someone else to turn to, a person they can open up with. I've got someone in mind, a man I think you'll get along with." He gave his cousin a firm look. "And I want you to go to the meetings. The white man's ways aren't all bad. Do the steps, okay?"

Vicente nodded. "I'll be in touch."

Ben climbed into the pickup, settling behind the wheel. He watched the pueblo diminish in the rearview mirror. Vicente stood still, raising one hand in a wave goodbye.

As the adobe buildings disappeared, Ben knew it was with him, part of every choice he'd make and every place he'd go. The eagle feather, his family, his traditions—they were all there, interwoven and inseparable.

The mountains rose and fell along the horizon, their

shapes shifting with the light. They were his guides, his landmarks, the steady giants that had framed his life for as long as he could remember.

He thought of the past week—Nathan's funeral, the cops and the lawyer, Zac's leaving, of the turmoil he still faced—but it all seemed less daunting now, somehow manageable. These last twenty-four hours, the ceremony, the words and warmth of family—they were part of his foundation, part of the new understanding that would guide him.

His state of near-euphoria, that profound inner peace, began to fray when he passed the spot on the highway where Raven and Nathan had died. He stopped the truck beside the road and got out, standing near the precipice to send a prayer outward. Although the gesture made him feel better, nothing would erase the loss.

And then there was the loss of Zac, his only child now, who would probably never return to live in the same home with Ben. He would do as Ben had, embrace his mother's tribe and grow up in their ways.

"Which is fine," Ben told himself as he returned to the truck and turned the key. "It's probably the right thing. But I miss him. I miss him like crazy."

He sat there another ten minutes, until cars began to slow and people to stare and wonder what was the problem. Finally, he took a long breath.

"Ben Pecos, you're a professional. You know how to handle grief and loss." But it was as he'd said to Julie, it felt so different when it was your own grief, your own family.

Another slow breath and he was on the road again. *I've got to get better at retaining the peace and calm of the ceremonial,* he lectured himself.

He called up memories of his childhood and his heritage, the foundation of his strength. As they returned to him now, they whispered of endurance, pushing him to remember that surrender was never an option. Each time his thoughts drifted to the police interrogations, the upcoming trial, he brought them back to those treasured memories.

He saw the soft glow of piñon wood burning in Grandmother's fireplace, felt the comfort of adobe walls cocooning him against the winter cold. The room was filled with a smoky warmth, her voice a steady rhythm in the circle of their family as she shared the traditional stories. She spoke of the deer spirit's grace, the buffalo's strength. In his mind, Ben was again the young boy sitting wide-eyed, absorbing these lessons like rain upon parched earth.

While the miles went by, his grandmother's words flowed back to him, recounting how the people endured through drought and hardship, always believing in the eventual return of abundance. Her stories were not merely tales but teachings, each one carrying the wisdom of generations. Ben could see his aunts nodding in agreement, the light of the fire dancing on their faces, reflecting a shared understanding. His grandmother had turned to him with a knowing look, her message clear: *perseverance is in your blood.*

Those memories were the essence of his upbringing, the strength he had drawn upon time and again. As at the ceremony this morning, the voices of his family formed a chorus in his mind, reminding him that, throughout history, they had faced challenges, had faced tragedy and despair, yet always held on. The clarity of these teachings resurfaced now, as if they had been waiting in the shadows to step forward when he needed them most. Ben felt them merging with Julie's words, both offering the same truth: *you are stronger than this.*

Giving up had never been part of his life, not when he'd first been sent away to Utah, not when his work took him to distant reservations, not when his mixed heritage made him question his place. And it wouldn't be part of him now. As the warmth of these memories seeped into him, Ben understood that they were more than comfort— they were a call to action. Surrender was not part of who he was. He could fight. He *would* fight.

At least the apartment wasn't far now. And then he'd be home, with Julie.

Chapter 32

Julie thumbed a text message back to Ben's note saying he was on the way back. Glad your Tewa time went so well. See you for lunch?

Heading down to the office when I get to town. Wanna set up my desk, even if I can't start work right away.

That was fine, she decided, although she'd been at loose ends ever since she handed over the threatening note and the strange gifts to Ron Parker last evening. She wandered into the kitchen, trying to decide whether she was hungry or not. Lunch with Ben would have been fun, especially if they headed over to Monroe's for their excellent beef burrito. Not as much fun on her own, so she made a quick sandwich instead.

She was two bites into it when her phone rang. She hoped Ben had changed his mind about lunch, but she saw the caller was Marie in Florida. Twice in a week? Maybe the friendship was going to take off as a long-distance one.

"Hey there! What's up?"

"I've only got a minute, Jules, but I had to give you a heads-up about something." Marie's tone was low and serious.

Julie took a deep breath. "Okay … Is this still about my article, the piece on Senator Landry?" Political exposés always carried some risk, usually to a journalist's reputation. "Don't tell me his office is starting a smear campaign against me. Cause, guess what? I don't work there anymore."

"This time I think you've kicked up something serious."

"What do you mean?"

"Scuttlebutt at the office says the senator's top aide was spotted in downtown Miami, the night before you filed your story, in a clandestine-looking conversation with a guy named Monty Carpaccio. They call him Monty the Snake."

Julie nearly laughed out loud, but something in her friend's tone told her this was serious. "What are you telling me, Marie?"

"I don't know. Just be careful. This guy is bad news. He was muscle for some pretty heavy players, went underground right after you and Ben moved away. They figured he was laying low till things cooled off."

Julie sank onto a chair and opened her laptop.

"He's not the only one out there, either," Marie added. "The editorial department has been warned away. These politicians are serious about keeping things buried."

A chill crept up her spine. "You're sure it's connected?" she pressed, needing the certainty only someone on the inside could give.

"Without a doubt. Julie, you've got to be careful. You don't want this kind of attention."

But Julie was already thinking three steps ahead. "Thanks, Marie. This helps. Really."

She hung up, staring at the screen in front of her where she'd typed Carpaccio's name. Marie was right. The guy had arrests going back twenty years, including for attempted murder in New York and extortion in DC.

The apartment felt suddenly empty. Julie sat alone at the dining table, buried in heavy thoughts. This was exactly the type of guy who would leave a threatening note on your windshield, she decided. Anything to scare her away from writing anything more, a blatant attempt to keep her quiet.

"If I'm right, we need to know who else is involved and how far they'll go." She rubbed her forehead. She'd known the senator's story was important, but … "This is bigger than I thought."

But the question remained—how had this Carpaccio managed to know where she was here in Albuquerque? And all that effort to warn her away by sticking a note on her car? He could have done that on the phone. Hell, he could have blasted her with emails and texts to get that message across. No, there was something more to it.

And Julie was going to figure it out.

She pulled out her phone and started to go through her notes. Her sandwich lay forgotten on the plate beside her laptop. She'd carefully made multiple copies of all of her research on Senator Landry, worried that losing her phone or wiping out her hard drive would mean the loss of all her months of hard work.

Landry, she'd discovered was headed for the top, and that meant offshore accounts, taking kickbacks and bribes, whatever it took to raise enough to launch a presidential run. Not this year, maybe not four years from now, but eventually he would be well-placed enough to do it, and in fine style with a huge war chest. Her research had been meticulous, as always, and she'd found a lot more than he wanted her to.

But Landry hadn't earned the nickname Slithering Russell for nothing. The man was an eel, able to slide out of any problem that came his way. She had no doubt he was doing it right now, calling together a team that would develop a strategy to discredit her and get away with his misdeeds.

On impulse, she closed out the notes section and opened her photos, tapping the main folder while she looked for the subfolder of items she'd photographed for the story. And there, among the most recent pictures she'd taken, were Zac and Nathan, a snapshot of life right before everything changed.

Her attention lingered on the two boys, arms thrown around each other's shoulders in carefree unity, standing in the parking lot at the Hotel Albuquerque the morning they were all leaving for Tewa. It seemed like a different lifetime now, a time when everything was simple, everyone alive. Her breath caught in her throat, memories of the boys.

And then her eyes widened as she noticed the cars in the background. She zoomed in, disbelief building as it hit her all at once. The U-Haul truck had been parked between her rental and Raven's sedan. It was gone in the photo because they'd delivered it to the storage place early that morning. And with the empty parking slot between them, she noticed for the first time how eerily similar her rental car was to Raven's compact sedan. Not exactly the same make and model, but so close.

Zooming in closer, it hit her right in the gut—the two out-of-state license plates were nearly alike. She recalled when she picked up the rental and teased herself that she always got an out-of-state car. But now she saw even more comparisons on the tags of the two cars—white background, a blue stripe of artwork across the top, red lettering. And the numbers were only a few digits apart. If someone had been told what car to look for in a crowded lot, it would have been easy to confuse these two.

Had Monty Carpaccio confused them?

The thought rocked her to the core, chilling and wild. She shook her head, trying to clear it. Could it be true? Her heartbeat thudded in her ears as she examined the photo again.

If this was what she suspected it was, if the tampered brakes were meant for her, the prosecutor's case against Ben would fall apart. Wouldn't it?

<h1 style="text-align:center">Chapter 33</h1>

Julie debated what to do—rather what to do *first*. She wanted to tell Ben, but she wanted to act upon the news, to have something more concrete to tell him. She reached for her sandwich and discovered a desiccated lump. When would she remember you couldn't leave bread out for hours in the dry air here? She tossed it in the trash and picked up her phone and purse.

She could drive down to Ben's new office, take some lunch for both of them, and show him her discovery in the photos. It would make so much more sense if he actually saw them. She recalled seeing a barbeque place on Carlisle, one that had a lot of cars in the lot. That seemed like a strong recommendation, so she headed in that direction, texting Ben to let him know her plan.

The first thing she noticed when she walked in the door

was the smell of barbeque so fabulous it made her knees weak, and a line of customers waiting to place orders. She stared at the to-go menu and immediately decided on pulled-pork sandwiches.

The second thing she noticed was the customer picking up his order, when he grabbed a bag and turned toward her. Detective Marcus Herrera. He recognized her right away—few people ever forgot her mane of red-gold curls.

He gave a curt nod and started to walk past, but Julie couldn't hold her enthusiasm. "Detective Herrera, wait. I've discovered something you really need to know."

He gave her a steady look, all the encouragement she needed.

"Look at my pictures. The two cars are similar, the plates nearly identical in color and design, and the numbers aren't that far apart either." She held up her phone. "Have you considered this angle?" she pressed, following as he walked toward the exit. "What if the car tampering wasn't meant for Raven? It might have been meant for me."

They were outside now, and the detective took a step back, skepticism still writ large across his face. "Mrs. Pecos, you're babbling. That's a big leap, even for you."

"But it's not impossible." She met his gaze, holding it steady, pouring every ounce of conviction into her stare.

He waved her off, and she realized she would get nowhere with this man. As far as he was concerned, he'd solved his case and arrested the killer. She gritted her teeth as she watched him walk away.

Jerk! Following him would accomplish nothing, she realized, so she turned back.

Twenty minutes later, with a bag of sandwiches and fries in hand, she walked into the building that housed

Ben's new office. His name wasn't on the door yet, one more reminder that he couldn't technically report for work until the upcoming trial went away.

She held up the fragrant food bag. "I brought one for Sandy, too. Forgot to ask if he was hungry."

"Oh, sorry. He's away on some other thing right now." Ben walked over and gave her a kiss. "That was so thoughtful, and I actually might be hungry enough to handle an extra."

He pulled out a chair and shoved some things aside so they could sit on opposite sides of his desk and spread out the feast. Before she'd taken more than three bites, Julie was already well into the story of her newest find.

"It makes a lot of sense," she said, picking up another fry. "Remember, the U-Haul truck was parked between the two compact white cars? It's probably what blocked the hotel's security camera from seeing Raven's car. Remember, they couldn't exactly explain why the camera didn't pick up someone messing with it."

"What's our next step?" Ben seemed to have forgotten about food. He'd taken one bite of his sandwich and none of the fries.

"Um, well …"

"Julie? What?"

"I think I kind of blew it with Detective Herrera."

"You went to his office?"

"No! It was a spontaneous thing." She explained about the chance meeting and how she'd blurted out what she'd discovered.

Ben stared. "You do realize he's kind of the enemy now. We need to let our attorney know, including the part you just told me."

Her mood fell. "You're right. We need to call her."

Ben picked up his phone and tapped the number. "Okay. Will do." He turned to Julie again. "She's in court. We have an appointment at five."

"Ben, I'm so sorry. I know better. I realize Marguerite and Ron Parker are the only ones we should be talking to. I blew it."

"Honey, don't do this." He circled the desk and tucked his forefinger under her chin, raising her face to look at him. "It doesn't sound like Herrera cares. Don't blame yourself. You did some amazing sleuthing this morning."

She gave a half-hearted smile, lunch forgotten on the desk.

"Hey, how about this … I don't have a pressing need to be here in the office. Let's get out of here. We'll take the food, and find a park where we can take a nice walk, spend some time outdoors before our meeting."

She nodded, only slightly mollified. While she packed up the sandwiches, Ben tidied the items on his desk and left a note for Sandy. They agreed to drive both vehicles back to the apartment and then walk to the park up the street, the same one that had felt so peaceful to Julie a few days ago.

* * *

"I still feel like such a dunce," Julie said as they tied the laces on their walking shoes. "What possessed me to talk to Herrera at all, much less reveal my information?"

"Leave it, at least for now. We'll see what Marguerite has to say. Right now, I feel like having a brisk walk and some fresh air." Ben's spirit perked up as they approached the park. Leaves whispered overhead, and the sun outlined a warm path along the walkways.

This world outside their apartment seemed to breathe hope into both of them. He found Julie's presence uplifting, her pace matching his long stride.

"Despite everything, I can't help but feel hopeful," she said. "I've spoken to one of my contacts, and she gave me a name."

"I knew you wouldn't be able to ignore your reporter instincts," he teased, watching the sparkle in her eyes.

"I might not be in the newsroom anymore, but I still have a few tricks up my sleeve," she replied with a grin.

Ben marveled at her ability to adapt and find ways to help even when the odds seemed stacked against them. She was considering angles he hadn't yet dreamed of.

"We'll find out who's behind this," he said.

"I know we will." Julie had a touch of steel in her tone.

"Thank you for believing in me, even when I was getting discouraged," Ben said, pulling her close as they reached the end of the path.

"It's what we do." Now she hoped the new information would come together as actual proof.

Chapter 34

It was 5:07 when Ben and Julie were escorted into Marguerite Ortiz's office. She looked tired. Apparently, this hadn't been an easy day for anyone. And the smile she sent toward them faded as Julie admitted her mistake in talking to the police.

Then, ever the professional, Marguerite took a long breath and sat up straight. "I'm impressed with the information you found. Send me those photos. Talking to Herrera wasn't wise, but you already know that. What I'll do is take your evidence directly to Dale Bachanda, the prosecutor, and strongly suggest that they drop the case against Ben."

Julie and Ben exchanged a glance. "That would be awesome," she said.

"Don't count on it working. The mix-up between the

two cars is still supposition, and we don't have an alternative suspect to sic them on."

"I might." Julie sat up straighter in her chair and told them about her conversation with her former colleague, Marie.

The attorney chewed at her lower lip for a moment. "Do we have evidence that this Monty Carpaccio is even in Albuquerque?"

"Nothing concrete yet."

"I'll get Ron Parker on it. He has an amazing number of contacts in the city, so we'll see what he can dig up."

"I gave Ron the threat note I received and a couple of unexplained items Ben and I found. He's checking them for fingerprints, so if this Carpaccio dude is in the system, maybe Ron will find a match."

"Let's hope so. Meanwhile, please keep in mind that if they followed you from Miami, we need to be extremely cautious." Marguerite's brow furrowed.

"What are our options?" Ben asked, his voice not quite steady.

Marguerite leaned back in her chair, considering. "Right now, the most important thing is to document everything. Every contact, every incident."

Julie nodded. She was already doing that.

The attorney's phone pinged with a message.

"That'll be the photos I forwarded to you," Julie informed her.

Marguerite opened the message and began scrolling through the pictures. "I see what you mean. This makes a lot of sense as an explanation." She stared toward the center of the room, tapping her nails on her desk. "I've got court all day again tomorrow, but I will put together a quick presentation to show to Bachanda. And I will talk to him—either tonight or at some point tomorrow. And then … we can only hope he'll see reason."

* * *

Never had an evening dragged so slowly. Ben and Julie went to bed but neither slept. Somewhere around two a.m. they got up and made hot chocolate. The sky was lightening over the top of Sandia Crest when they drifted off to sleep.

At eight o'clock Ben's phone rang, jarring them both.

"It's Marguerite," he said, clearing his throat and rubbing his face before picking up. He swiped to take the call and hit the speaker button at the same time.

"Bachanda refuses to drop the charges. Thought I'd better give it to you straight. It's pretty much for the reasons we talked about, plus the guy's lazy. And he knows Herrera's lazy. Anybody that close to retirement doesn't want to shake things up."

"So, what do we do?" Ben asked, sitting up in bed and rubbing his forehead.

"I'm due in the courtroom in fifteen minutes. But I've got a message out to Ron Parker. I'd like for you two to meet with Ron and me in my office again. It'll be late afternoon, kind of like yesterday, if you're available."

"Let me check my busy calendar," Ben said, the jest falling flat.

"We'll be there," Julie added. "Whatever it takes, we're going to clear Ben's name."

The call ended and they looked at each other. "Well. That's that." Ben said. He set the phone on his nightstand and rolled over.

Julie lay there, too alert to close her eyes.

* * *

Ron Parker was walking toward Marguerite's office door at the same time Ben and Julie arrived.

"Eventful day, huh," he commented, waiting at the bottom step of the porch until they caught up.

"You could say that." Ben seemed in a better humor, Julie thought. He should. He'd slept at least six hours after the attorney's call this morning. They'd spent the rest of the day at their new house, measuring for window coverings and furniture, pleased to see how well the contractor's crew was moving along. Anything to pass the time without hanging around the apartment.

"Oh, I've got something for you," Ron said to Julie, reaching into his jacket and pulling out the items he'd borrowed, the carved alligator and the photo of Zac. "No fingerprints showed up on either, other than yours and mine."

They walked in, past the reception desk, and into the conference room near the back. Marguerite was waiting. She reached out and pulled Julie into a hug. "I'm so sorry I wasn't able to deliver better news this morning."

Julie nodded, setting her things on the table and walking to the sideboard for a glass of water.

"Okay, folks, fill me in. I'm hoping something magical happened while I was in court all day." Marguerite sat at the head of the table, kicking off her shoes and opening their file.

Ron spoke up, his voice calm and focused. "I've already started looking into this Monty Carpaccio's New Mexico connections. He wasn't only hiding out. He's been busy taking on a side job or two, according to scuttlebutt on the street."

Julie felt a chill. "Like what?"

"My informant says he'll do anything from extortion to petty theft. More of the latter in recent days," Ron replied. "But he's smart. Moves around a lot. Keeps a low profile."

Julie nodded. "That fits with what I've heard."

Ron nodded. "If I had to guess, he's hanging out here, waiting for orders. Otherwise, he would've done what they paid him to and gotten out of the state."

"You mean he's probably coming after me again?" Julie's freckles stood out against her pale skin.

"Your theory makes sense, that you're the one he was after. He tried, got the wrong person, then he left you a warning note, hoping to scare you off."

Marguerite tapped a pencil on the table, lost in thought. "The fact that you know this much already puts you in danger, but it also gives us leverage. If they think you're too close, they may act quickly."

Ben frowned. "So, we're dealing with a timeline, too."

"Yes," Marguerite said. "And not in our favor." She paused, eyes narrowing. "I assume you're still set on pursuing this?"

Julie looked at Ben, saw his steadying support. "We don't have a choice. Ben can't go on trial for murder."

Marguerite's expression softened slightly. "Then we play it smart. Ron, can you keep an eye out for the suspect?"

Ron nodded. "Already got people working on it. If he makes a move, we'll know." He picked up the carved alligator, fiddling with it, staring at the pattern in the wood.

"Meanwhile, Julie, I need you to be extremely careful," Marguerite continued. "Don't take unnecessary risks. And don't be alone, if you can help it."

"I won't," Julie promised. But her mind was already spinning with plans.

Ron, the only one of them who couldn't sit still, paced the length of the room. "We need to set up a trap to catch this thug at something."

"Wh—"

He held up a palm. "Think about it. The accident happened outside the city, and the state police handled that investigation and arrested Ben. But if we get this Carpaccio dude and catch him committing a crime within the city limits, it's APD who'll have him. And I've got some friends in the department who'll take me seriously when I let them know the background."

Julie took a deep breath. "That's brilliant."

"And how do you propose we catch him in a crime?" Ben asked. "Anyone this desperate might be looking over their shoulders, or he could get orders to strike again right away. We have to put this in motion quickly."

"You're right, Ben," Ron replied. "They know who you are, and the clock is ticking, especially if it's true that Julie's story about Senator Landry is what started this whole thing." In his enthusiasm, the carved alligator went flying and hit the doorjamb. "Oops, sorry about that."

Julie slid out of her chair and retrieved it. "Oh. Looks like the tail broke off." She held the two pieces, fitting them together, but the wooden piece would need glue.

"Hold on a second," Ron said, stopping beside her. "Let me see that."

A phone pinged, grabbing Ben's attention. He saw his own phone vibrating on the table and hesitated for a moment before answering. The name on the display alarmed him. He stood quickly and motioned to the others. "I need to take this call," he said. He moved to the other room.

Ben sat on the edge of the reception desk, rubbing his

temple with his free hand. "I'm glad you called, Vicente. What's up?" He pushed aside the troubles waiting for him in the other room, focusing on his cousin's faltering words.

"I didn't want anyone to know, especially my mom. I slipped. Used coke again this afternoon." Vicente's voice cracked.

Ben had spoken with Sandy and passed along several names to Vicente, including a group that met at the church at Tewa. He wondered why Vicente hadn't called his sponsor. "Have you attended meetings? Started working with someone?"

A long silence followed. Ben worried the call had dropped. "I went to a meeting, met some people. Then, when I left, my old supplier was standing there, right by the basketball court. I … I'm so screwed up, Ben. I thought I could talk to him for only a minute, that I could handle it."

The admission felt heavy, and Ben knew Vicente well enough to understand how hard this was for him. This was different, like nothing Ben had heard from him before. There was no hint of the arrogance or dismissiveness his cousin often used to mask his emotions. It was laid out with no excuses to hide behind.

He leaned back, letting his own thoughts slow and settle. He was torn between his professional instincts as a psychologist and the pull of family bonds, and he wondered if his advice was going to be colored by which side of himself he was listening to.

"What you say in the meetings is private. *We'll* keep it private. Please don't back out now."

The line was quiet again, but this time Ben felt hope in Vicente's silence.

"Okay," his cousin finally said. "Okay."

"I'll call you tomorrow, early." Ben paused, making sure his words had sunk in. "Hang in there." He put the phone down and stared at it, as if it might start ringing again. His mind felt stretched and thin, like too little fabric over too many obligations.

This was his cousin, practically a brother to him, and Ben couldn't stand the thought of letting him slip away. His promise was real, but he also understood that even with his training and experience, there were some promises that couldn't be kept without the other person meeting him halfway.

When Ben rejoined the others in Marguerite's conference room, Ron was taking the tip of a pocketknife to the alligator figurine. He pulled out a metal button, about a half-inch in diameter. "Well, well."

"What's that?" The question was on everyone's lips, but Julie was the one to say it.

"A tracker." Ron's mouth formed a tight, straight line. "This explains a lot."

The answers came together in one blinding swoop. It was obvious how the thug had known where the car was in the hotel parking lot. With the alligator carving packed among their household possessions and his orders to disable a white compact car, he'd shown up to do the job. With one fatal mistake. Wrong white car, wrong out-of-state license plate.

"And once we moved into the apartment, he knew exactly where we lived." Ben felt sick as Julie put the pieces together for the group.

"The white car was gone by then, returned to the rental place," she said. "Did he find my new Toyota—"

"Probably by watching us come and go." He reached

across the table and took her hand. "My God, that's scary." He looked toward Ron. "Is that thing still working?"

"It doesn't have a blinking light or anything," the PI informed them, "but my guess is yes. It didn't sustain much of a blow when the tail broke loose from the main part of the carving. We should treat it as if it is."

"And …?"

Ron smiled. "I think we can use it to set a trap, catch us a killer." He proceeded to outline a plan.

Chapter 35

By noon the next day, Julie had made calls and sent emails to Miami. "My editor at the *Herald* practically salivated when I told him I had a follow-up to my original story. Anything that lands reprints in major papers and headline news exposés on TV is going to grab his attention."

Now, as the sun edged lower in the west, Julie's notebook was open in front of her, covered in hastily scribbled names. She gave the assembled group a reassuring nod. "All according to plan. We're putting out the word that we've solved Raven's death and that the killer has named people high up in national politics as being behind it. Trust me, politicians are super sensitive to anything involving Natives and their culture. If … okay I'll say *when* such a story gets out, DC will have people scrambling to cover their … assets."

Ron had also dropped the word on the streets of Albuquerque. The nosy reporter knew Carpaccio's name and was about to file an even bigger story than her first one.

"It's either going to send him so far into hiding that no one will ever find him, or he'll come looking for you, Julie, wanting to get rid of you and your research before you can publish that story." Ron's comment didn't ease Ben's mind one bit. "If it's the latter, he'll probably be acting on orders from higher up."

"It'll spook him or it'll scare the hell out of the DC contingent," Ben said. "That might work." He leaned back, resisting the urge to bite his nails.

"Nothing starts a panic like too much attention from nosy reporters." Ron glanced at Julie, sending a subtle wink.

Ben focused on the thin thread of evidence they had started pulling when they realized how imminent the danger was. The whole scenario had sounded like a distant, made-up nightmare when it first came crashing into their lives. And somewhere, now, was Ben's uneasy center, the part of him that pulled in different directions. He'd never had trouble navigating between the worlds he occupied. Between Tewa and Anglo, between psychologist and family man. But now it all felt different. There was more at stake. And his fear that even his best efforts might not be enough drove him in ways that surprised even him.

Julie's vehicle was parked outside Marguerite's office, a clear signal that she was inside. What wasn't so evident were the butterflies in her stomach. She'd planted the story idea with her editor, gotten the rumor mill whirling. Ron walked in with a woman he introduced as his sister, Charlie Parker.

She was close to Julie's age, casual in jeans, a bright turquoise t-shirt, and denim jacket, with an auburn ponytail. Ron was right—Julie liked her immediately when Charlie set a huge bag of takeout meals from a place called Pedro's on the table.

"Green chile chicken enchiladas for dinner," she announced. "We've gotta start feeding you guys right."

Ron was going over the plan with Ben. Outside surveillance in place—check. Cameras hidden around the conference room—check. Communication systems tested and operational—check. "When I spread the word in the parts of town where we think Carpaccio's been hanging out, talking about the break in the story, I said Julie was using borrowed office space because she was spooked about working from home."

"He'll think he's outsmarting us by finding you here at Marguerite's place, since he doesn't know that we know about the tracker," Charlie offered. All eyes went to the conference table where the broken alligator carving sat, its electronic guts exposed.

"Where's Marguerite?" Ben asked, realizing he hadn't seen the attorney since they arrived.

"She went home." Ron circled the room, making sure the shutters at each window were tightly closed. "I suggested she stay away, and she was okay with that. I didn't want her walking in here at the wrong moment, potentially getting caught in the crossfire."

"Crossfire? Do you think this thug will be armed?" There went those butterflies again.

"His history is more sneaky than violent, but we can't rule out anything. We don't know what he's been ordered to do." Charlie lifted the back of her jacket to reveal a pistol in her waistband.

Ron passed around a sheet with mug shots and a short version of Carpaccio's rap sheet. "And don't worry about your vehicle—one of the APD officers is right behind the hedge out there, keeping an eye to be sure this guy doesn't try his old tricks with the brakes."

They took seats around the table, opening the boxed dinners and inhaling the fragrant chile aroma. Ben glanced over at Julie, watching as she gnawed a fingernail, brow furrowed and deep in thought. "You're not supposed to be worrying," he said softly.

Julie's head jerked up, a glint in her eyes. "When the man I'm married to is acting as the bait in a trap, you bet I'm going to worry."

She was afraid, and Ben couldn't blame her. They'd already agreed that it should appear from the outside as though Julie was in here alone, but in reality, it would be Ben in the room when their suspect walked in, following the tracker's locator signal.

She looked at Ron. "How sure are you that Carpaccio won't sniff out the trap?"

"He's working with limited info, which means we control the narrative. Ben will be the first one he sees—you do have that vest on, right?" At his nod, Ron continued. "The rest of us will be monitoring from Marguerite's private office and we'll have the suspect's exit cut off from the moment he walks into the building."

Ben felt the full responsibility, knowing any mistake would be his fault. He turned to Julie. "I need to know you're not gonna worry," he said, hating the fear that flickered across her face.

"You could stop my worry," she said. Her words were

calm, but her tone left no room for argument. "You could let someone else be the bait."

He swallowed hard, the muscles in his jaw twitching. This was turning into the one thing he hadn't wanted it to: personal.

Charlie gave a *hm-hm* sound. "We should eat while we can and then make this place look like there's only one person in the building. Right?"

It made sense, and no one wanted those enchiladas to go to waste. They passed out the containers and plastic cutlery. "They're a whole lot better with a margarita," Charlie joked.

"Shh," Ron hissed. He had two fingers up to his left ear where he wore a tiny comm device. "Shit!"

He grabbed his food container and snapped it shut. "Quick, gather everything. Ben, it's showtime. The rest of us need to get across the hall asap."

"What—"

"Outside surveillance spotted a male subject circling the building, approaching the back window at the kitchen."

Ben felt a knot tighten in his chest. He patted the Kevlar vest under his shirt.

"Ben?" Julie asked the question without speaking, searching for assurance that things would go their way.

He wanted to say he was sure, to promise they'd get through it unscathed, to claim it would all be a terrible memory by next week. He squeezed her hand and gave her a quick kiss on the cheek.

Ron and Charlie had gathered all the food containers—a dead giveaway to their presence—and were at the door. "Ben, switch on the cameras we rigged. And remember, that Kevlar is not invincible."

As they slipped across the hall, Charlie's hand firmly on Julie's shoulder, Ben's gut tensed. He watched Julie slip into Marguerite's office with more reluctance than he'd ever seen from her, an unspoken "be careful" hanging between them.

They'd come up with the best plan they could, given the hand they were dealt. His job now was to see it through. He walked over to the file cabinet and switched on one of the cameras, then the other one nestled on a bookcase. Now, Ron and at least one of the cops outside could monitor what was going on in the room. It was small comfort.

Taking a seat at the table and acting calm was the hardest thing he'd ever done.

And then he heard a small *thump*, coming from the other side of the wall from where he was sitting.

Chapter 36

He thought of the backup that surrounded him—cops outside, Ron and Charlie across the hall, keeping Julie safe. But the reassurance did nothing to stop the pounding in his ears as he detected stealthy footsteps moving along the hall outside this room. The building had purposely been left in darkness, other than this room to act as a beacon for the intruder.

It worked. The door swung open, and a slight, male figure stepped in. Ben felt an initial jolt of surprise, not expecting the man to be so thin, almost wiry, and much older than he'd guessed from the mugshot photos. He locked eyes with him; he would not be the first to look away. "I'm Ben Pecos," he said, voice steady.

And then he saw the knife. And the thug's expression turned wary. His eyes darted to the shuttered window and to the papers on the table and finally back to Ben. "They said there'd be a woman here," he said, a slight quaver in his voice.

"She's the reason we're meeting," Ben said. "So is this." He slid the slim folder across the table, every move geared toward the purpose of recording what happened. "Have a seat and let's talk."

The man looked from the file to Ben, ignoring the invitation. "You with the cops or something?" He glanced toward the door, nervous energy crackling in the air.

"Something. It's not hard to figure out who I am. You've been trailing my wife." The statement drew a shift in the man's posture, and Ben knew they were right. "There are witnesses and video surveillance that show you tampering with the brakes on a car. Only problem is that you got the wrong car and killed two innocent people."

Carpaccio's open mouth betrayed shock at that news. But he quickly recovered his bluster. "You people don't even know who you're dealing with. If you think arresting me will make a difference, you don't know a damn thing."

Ben nodded slowly, staying focused on the thug. "Sure, sure," he said. "We don't know anything, so why don't you explain?"

The suspect backed toward the door, but Ron Parker had materialized there and he snatched the knife from Carpaccio's hand before the man could react.

"There's nothing to explain," he said, shifting uneasily and turning back toward Ben, suddenly desperate for a quick solution.

Ben kept cool and calm, knowing the plan was going off-script and careful not to let that change the end result.

Ron stepped fully into the room, edging the thug up

against the conference table. "Got a few questions, since you're already here," he said, unfazed by the man's attempt to leave. "Who hired you, and why did they think Julie Conlin needed more than a scare?"

Ben stayed quiet, trusting Ron to ask the right questions, the facts the prosecution team would need.

"Nobody hired me," Carpaccio said, a look of forced confidence crossing his features. "What the hell do you think this is, some reality show? Go back to your paperwork, Pecos."

Ben rose from his chair, making sure not to block the cameras. "I think this is a bigger deal than you're used to," he said. "I think you're desperate enough to admit it."

The man shifted again, his bravado melting away as Ben closed in, his six-foot frame towering over the smaller man. He threw a quick glance at Ron, knowing they had him cornered.

"I don't know anything," he said. "You can't pin a thing on me."

"About the car," Ben said, his voice edged with emotion. "Who did it, and why?"

A tense silence, then the man blinked. "I—" he started, voice catching in his throat.

Ben saw it in the man's face, knowing he was close, knowing they had him. "Who ordered the tampering with the brakes?"

The thug's expression shifted, going from confidence to panic in a single moment. "I don't know!" he shouted, the words tumbling from his mouth. "Nobody tells me! They just said to make it look like an accident. Honest to God." He swallowed hard, resignation settling on him as he spoke again. "I just did what I was told."

Ben's heart thudded as he processed the confession. It wasn't an act of random violence. They'd been right. Julie was the target, and the stakes were higher than they'd guessed.

Ron stepped toward the man, his voice low and insistent. "Give us a name. And think about it first, 'cause this is your last chance."

The man hesitated, his reluctance painful. "I told you," he said finally, though his tone carried more defeat than defiance. "Nobody tells me anything. They only—"

Julie stepped into the room. "Keep talking," she said. "Make this quick for all of us."

The thug looked from her to Ben and finally back to Ron. "There's some guy named Smith. I swear that's all I know."

"Smith? How conveniently generic." This time it was Charlie, who'd stepped into the doorway. Out of sight of the cameras, she'd drawn her pistol.

"Okay, okay. Smith has dropped the names of somebody called Jake Flowers, and a Mr. L. I swear those are the only ones I've heard. I didn't want to—"

"Jake Flowers … he's one of Landry's top aides." Julie didn't seem especially surprised.

"Senator Landry," Ben said, fitting the pieces together. "A politician. Damn." The connection was painfully clear now, and so was the motive. Julie's exposé had been spot-on.

But his firecracker wife wasn't done with this thug. "Okay, you were told to get rid of me—I get that. And I fully understand why. But the timing … I'd already filed my story. It was due to hit the headlines. Your cutting the brake lines on the car wouldn't have stopped that. Why would you take the chance for some corrupt politician, when it wasn't going to make a difference anyway?"

Carpaccio looked like he wanted to strangle her, but Ben took a menacing step forward and the thug backed away and slumped into a chair. "I blew it."

"What do you mean?" Julie was in full reporter mode now.

"I was supposed to get to you a lot earlier, back in Florida."

"And …?"

"The damn hurricane messed me up. I'd been watching your house, even found a chance to puncture the brake line on your car while it sat in your driveway. You'd go out the next day, get on the interstate, and after a few miles when you got up to speed, that tiny leak of brake fluid would leave you without stopping power, right about the time you got up to seventy miles an hour."

"And the hurricane hit our place, trashing the house and sending a huge tree across the driveway and taking out both of our cars." She actually laughed at that.

Carpaccio had the good grace to realize the irony of his blunder. "Yeah, well. And then it became obvious you two were moving away. The U-Haul truck, all those packing boxes, and I had no idea where you'd go. So, I planted a couple trackers in your stuff."

Ben had a puzzled frown on his face. "But that means you could have caught up with the U-Haul anywhere along the road."

"Yes, but I couldn't catch up with Miss Reporter here because she wasn't with you in the truck, was she? And I was already on the road behind you. Got as far as Tallahassee before I knew for a fact that you were alone in the truck."

"And in your brilliant little mind you figured it out—you'd have to follow Ben until wherever he caught up with his wife." Charlie had lowered the pistol but she was right there, piecing it together.

"And it turned out that was Albuquerque freaking New Mexico," the thug complained. "My trackers got me to the hotel, and one of the senator's aides had somehow figured out that Julie Conlin rented—"

"A white sedan with a blue-on-white motif license plate."

He nodded. "It was parked right by the damn U-Haul. How was I to know there were two of those in the same parking lot?"

By looking more carefully, Ben thought. But then, if Carpaccio had done his homework, he and Julie would be lying dead at the bottom of the drop-off on the way to Tewa Pueblo. He felt his throat tighten at the prospect.

"Okay, so I've got a question," Charlie said, stepping into the room. "Why didn't you simply disappear? You're clear across the country from all that drama on the east coast, why wait around here and keep coming after Julie?"

Carpaccio slumped in his seat, dropping his head to his hands. "They've got my granddaughter."

"What?" Four faces registered stunned surprise.

"I tell you, Landry plays for keeps and there's no loose ends when he wants something done. I don't know if it's the senator himself or his top aides, or who's calling the shots … but I was told that until I supply proof that Julie Conlin Pecos, the award-winning journalist, was dead, my six-year-old grandchild is at their mercy."

"But … I'd already filed my story. The damage was

done. Was this some kind of retribution by Landry?"

"I don't know. Don't really care. I just want Lila back."

"And you planned to do this … how?"

Carpaccio reached into his pocket and pulled out a note. Julie took it and read the typed words aloud. "I'm so sorry for ruining the life of an innocent man. Senator Landry was the victim of a malicious news story, and I'm to blame."

She stared at the thug. "What. The. Hell!"

Ben thought she was about to jump on Carpaccio and strangle him. He laid a hand on her arm as a gentle reminder that there were cameras and recorders in the room.

"As soon as I confirmed you were dead, the note would go out to the media." Another shrug. "Seemed like an answer that could make everybody happy."

This time, Ben wanted to strangle him. But Ron was already speaking into his comm device and four police officers converged on the scene. As everyone else stepped out of the way, the Albuquerque Police Department took over, handcuffing the man and reading him his rights.

"Call me a lawyer," the thug said as they closed in. His voice was resigned, his words now nearly a whisper.

Ron and one of the officers circled the room, collecting the ironclad evidence that would put away this small-time creep plus a few rather important people in the nation's capital.

Chapter 37

Ben sat quietly in his office, the dim light casting shadows across the room at the end of a long day. A low hum from the heating system provided white noise that matched his mood. Ben stared at the ceiling, but all he saw was Raven's terrified face and Nathan's blank, lifeless eyes. The memories crashed over him.

It's part of the grieving process, he reminded himself, the waves of sadness that pop up at the oddest times. He had everything to be happy and grateful for—Julie was safe, his new job could now begin, and he was close to his Tewa family once again. There was no logical reason for this funk. But then, emotions weren't always logical.

A tap sounded on the doorframe. "Hey, Ben." Sandy's head peeked around the corner. "Got a minute?"

"Lots of minutes, right now."

"You okay?" Sandy stepped into the office and sat in the chair across the desk from Ben.

A quick nod. "Yeah. Doing too much thinking."

Sandy nodded, his gaze focused downward. "It's been less than a month since they died."

How did his old friend know exactly what was on his mind? "Was it that evident from my face?"

"Ever since the police arrested that thug last week, I've noticed only two expressions on your face, my friend. The smiley version is a reminder that you and Julie are safe now. The distressed version means you're still thinking about the accident. You lost an adopted son, Ben. That doesn't quickly go away. It never goes away."

"I can't believe how much I'm thinking about Raven, too. Her strength, how she never wavered. Both boys looked up to her, and she was a good mother." The pain of losing them settled deeper, despite every rational thought that told him none of what happened was his fault. "I guess the part that eats at me is that I didn't love Raven—admired her, yes. But you know that Julie is the love of my life."

"I know, Ben. I know. And that shouldn't be a source of guilt."

Ben rubbed his temples, recalling his mother's voice, the comfort of her Tewa accent that now whispered in his memory. He knew how these things worked, how guilt could consume, twist, and distort until the truth became unrecognizable. But knowing didn't lessen the pain; it only amplified it.

He turned to Sandy. "You've been so patient with me, waiting while I went through all this … this drama."

Sandy waved away the compliment. "Time is what you needed."

"My grandmother taught me so much. I can hear her voice as soft as the wind through cottonwoods. She told me a child couldn't run from hard things, couldn't hide and wait for them to pass. She taught me to stand like the sunflowers, with heads turned bravely to the sky." He took a deep breath. "And even though I have all these thoughts about Raven and Nathan, and although I miss Zac and fear that I've lost him too, I know that hiding and waiting for it to pass isn't the answer."

Sandy nodded. "Your grandmother was a wise woman. Something will show Zac that you still love him and won't give up. But pushing the matter isn't what it takes."

"I know. I've even had the thought of flying up to Moose Flats, surprising him at the village. Being there for him, like I promised when Zac left with Rynah and E.J." He rubbed his left eyebrow. "But it's too soon. He needs to settle in, go back to his Haida life, raising his dogs, finishing school ..."

"And one day he'll be back here to see you again. Give him the time he needs. Give yourself more time, Ben."

"It's hard, not pushing to see him, but you're right. Someday I'll find the words to reach Zac, to show him we still have a future." Ben let out a long breath. This was what he knew—connection, healing. He thought of Vicente, who'd stayed clean for a full week now. Baby steps. This was what he did best.

"Use the same patience and care you've learned as a counselor, the same gentle techniques that bring other people back to hope."

If he could help strangers find their way, he could do the same for Zac. For himself. He wouldn't let the tragedy define them, wouldn't let it tear them apart. He felt the purpose flood back, driving him to action. He'd reach Zac, he'd rebuild.

"Right now, Sandy, I need to get back to work. I need to work with people, renew my skills as a counselor, and see the positives again."

Sandy smiled wide, his relief evident. "So many of the pueblo people could use help, Ben. I've been pulling case files and can send you pretty much anyplace you want to go. We should sit down together, discuss and evaluate, and then you can choose where to go first. Shall we start on it first thing Monday?"

Ben nodded. "Monday is great."

Sandy left the room, and Ben walked over to the window, staring out at the city lights beyond, digesting the conversation. Then he stepped into the hallway, letting the door close softly behind him, a punctuation mark on his decision.

Chapter 38

Ben and Julie wrestled the last two boxes from the back of Ben's pickup truck and into their new Albuquerque house on November first. A cardboard forest had already overtaken the living room, not to mention multiple deliveries from American Furniture, Amazon, and a few other online shopping sites. Bless Julie, she had coordinated all the shipments so everything would arrive while they still had the energy to deal with it. The mountain of belongings felt insurmountable, but this was the last of it.

Ben set his box on the floor and read its label aloud: "Memories." A long breath slipped from his lips. He looked over at Julie, who swept a tangle of hair from her freckled face as she lifted a box that was destined for her home office. The long drive from Florida and the move were behind them. So were all the hurricanes, the legal hassles, and most of the qualms.

Their physical exhaustion was overshadowed by relief. Closing the front door felt like slamming shut a chapter of their lives, one filled with turmoil. Now, they were here, in this house with its promise of peace and new beginnings.

Sunlight filtered through the half-open blinds, casting stripes across the scattered boxes. Ben felt the weight of their journey begin to lift, replaced by a sense of accomplishment and his excitement about the job he'd started last week.

"We made it," Julie said, her voice a blend of disbelief and triumph.

Ben nodded, sinking onto the edge of a couch covered in its protective shipping plastic. "I can't believe it's real," he replied. "After this last month of sheer turmoil, I kept thinking something else would come up."

Julie sat beside him, her fingers lacing with his. "Nothing left but this," she said softly, leaning her head on his shoulder.

Ben glanced around at the maze of boxes and let out a tired laugh. "A few memories to unpack."

"We can do it," Julie replied, slapping both knees and leaping up. "We're starting fresh, here together." She disappeared into the kitchen.

A moment later, Ben heard the sliding thud of a window opening, followed by a rush of cold air. It swept through the house like a balm, a clean and exhilarating chill. Ben stood and followed, drawn to her as he had always been, finding her by the sink, breathing deeply, soaking in the scent of frosty autumn leaves and the huge spruce tree in the backyard. She looked like the Julie he had known before the chaos: calm, resilient, ready.

Julie opened her eyes and smiled at him. "This is exactly

what I needed."

He walked over, wrapping his arms around her. "Fresh air?"

She laughed, a warm, light sound that filled the space. "And you. Us."

Ben held her close, savoring the warmth between them. "We've been through a lot," he said. "I wasn't sure we'd get here."

"I know," she replied, her voice soft with remembrance. "But we did. And now we have this chance to start over."

Ben kissed her forehead, grateful.

"This is our fresh start," Julie said, leaning against him, staring toward the western horizon.

He nodded. "And it's going to be great."

Julie turned her attention to the box nearest her feet, labeled "Kitchen." She pulled at the tape and opened the flaps, unwrapping each item with deliberate care. A mug came loose in Julie's hands, one with a *Miami Herald* logo—a memento of the work she'd poured herself into, but also a reminder of the relentless pace and the emotional toll. She placed the mug in a cupboard, taking a breath, considering her decision to leave the news behind, as she'd left the last couple months' upheaval behind.

Ben leaned against the counter. "What are you thinking?"

"I want to do something different," she admitted. "The work I've done, it feels … important, but I'm feeling worn out. I'm not sure I want to keep chasing stories like that. And I've decided I hate politics."

"You've always said you wanted to make a real impact. What are you thinking of now?"

She picked up another mug, this one plain and simple.

"Something meaningful here," she said, her voice firmer. "Maybe projects that connect people. Something positive for the pueblo community. I'm ready for a change."

Ben nodded. "Whatever you do, you'll be great at it."

"It'll be different, a real change," Julie said, a hint of excitement in her voice. "But I think it's exactly what I need."

"And what you deserve," Ben added, reflecting on how they could both contribute to something bigger than themselves.

She finished putting away the mugs and glassware, handed him the empty box, and reached into another. "I've always loved the way you bring people together," Julie said. "What about events that focus on cultural storytelling?"

Ben nodded, considering her proposal. "There are so many elders with stories to tell, and very few published books on the subject. We could organize something where they share them with the younger generation."

Julie's excitement glowed. "Yes! And maybe tie in some writing workshops. You know, for kids who want to turn those stories into books or articles."

Ben admired her ability to dream while keeping the interests of the community in focus. "What if we became involved in cultural exchange programs too? In addition to the major events, such as the intertribal powwows or the Gathering of Nations," he suggested. "You could invite artists and storytellers from other pueblos, or even other indigenous communities."

"I need to tread carefully, make sure those things would be welcome, especially coming from an Anglo. But it could be amazing. With some interviews, pieces that highlight the work being done by the puebloans, especially the kids, it could bring attention to the unbelievably rich culture and art scene here."

Ben thought of Vicente and his desire to create pottery.

As they continued to build on each other's vision, Ben told her more about his summers at the pueblo with his grandmother and aunts, how his life had been a bridge between two worlds.

Now, that bridge was a strength, a means to connect different communities and approaches. He saw their involvement as an extension of his heritage and Julie's skills, a way to honor both and make a meaningful impact. This was how they worked best: side by side, partners in every sense. Ben marveled at how this moment of quiet togetherness felt, especially after the anguish of recent months—losses and renewal, over and over.

Within an hour, empty boxes littered the floor, and Ben slit the tape and flattened them for the recycling center. Julie had made excellent progress at finding places for everything in the new kitchen. She brushed her hands against her jeans and reached for the last box, labeled "Glassware."

As she pulled out their best wine glasses, she spotted a wrapped parcel. For one frightening instant, she had a flashback. But this one was covered in beautiful floral paper and had a note taped to it, with familiar handwriting. The note read, *Distance can't keep true friends apart. Follow your dreams!*

"Aww … Ben, look at this."

He joined her, curious. "What is it?"

She unwrapped the box, revealing a handmade dreamcatcher. "A gift from Marianne," Julie said, smiling as she recognized the handiwork. "She must have slipped it in before we left."

Ben remembered their friends back in Florida, the way they had rallied around them through the hurricane destruction and their decision to move away. "That's so like her," he said. "Always thoughtful."

Julie read the note again, her expression softening. "It's a nice reminder. Even though we're not there anymore, we still have so much support."

The ornament was a symbolic protective charm, meant to keep bad dreams away while letting good dreams pass through. "It's perfect, as if Marianne knew in advance about the conversation we'd be having today."

Julie hung the dreamcatcher on the French door leading to the backyard, in a place she would see every day, its presence a cheerful reminder of their ties across the miles.

"We've worked hard enough for one day," Julie announced. "I'm going to find that nice bottle of wine Sandy gave us, make a snack to go along with it, and we're going to relax."

"First, one other thing." Ben was standing at the living room window, looking into the distance. "Put on your jacket. You've gotta see this."

The last rays of sunlight clung to the western sky in shades of magenta and gold, a dazzling show that marked the end of one day and the promise of another. Julie set down the wine bottle and joined him on the front lawn.

"We came a long way to reach this point, didn't we?" She looped her arm through his.

"I love the feel of this new future that's calling out to us." Down inside his coat pocket, his phone rang. "Hm, speaking of something calling out ..." He looked at the screen and eagerly took the call.

The young voice hesitated. "Dad? What are you guys doing at Christmas?"

A lump formed in Ben's throat, and Julie snuggled in close as a plan came together. When he put his phone away, Ben blinked hard. He knew this was only the beginning, and he couldn't wait to see it unfold.

Author notes:

As I've told my newsletter readers, this book was truly a labor of love for me. My dear friend Susan Slater created the Ben Pecos series and characters (along with the Dan Mahoney mystery series, and several standalone novels), and she entrusted me with their care after her death. When she first told me she was planning to do this, I wept. So honored. She only lived a few months after her cancer diagnosis, and we shared several conversations and many emails, discussing plans for keeping her books in print and continuing her life's work. *The Homecoming* is the tenth book in the Pecos series, my first. Thank you, Susan, for giving me this opportunity.

I've set more than 40 of my own novels here in my home state, but this was my first experience at writing an

American Indian protagonist and delving into the native culture. Believe me, it was a bit intimidating!

I want to thank Sarah Elisabeth Sawyer, Choctaw tribal member from Texas and Oklahoma, for her words of wisdom on writing about American Indian cultures. Sarah taught me so many things: preferred terminology, the finer points of writing about another culture, her emphasis on what may be shared and what things are considered sacred and private. I've worked to accomplish this, and hope I haven't made too many blunders. Anne Hillerman also offered words of encouragement in this endeavor. She and Susan were good friends for many years, and Anne's dad, Tony, was one of Susan's early mentors when she began writing this series. And finally, to the late Joe Sando of Jemez Pueblo, I owe so much. Sando's work helped me fill so many gaps in my basic knowledge of the 19 Pueblos of Northern New Mexico. Given all of these supporters, I hope I have done the work justice.

Approaching the finish line, as always, I'm forever grateful to my editor at Secret Staircase Books, Stephanie Dewey and her fantastic team of beta readers: Eve Osborne, Susan Gross, Marcia Koopmann, Isobel Tamney, Paula Webb, and Sandra Anderson. You're so good at catching the little things I overlook after reading a book a thousand times. A huge thanks to all—you have my undying gratitude!

What's next for Ben Pecos?

It's their first New Mexico Christmas as a family, and Ben wants to make it a special one for Zac's visit. But when the teen shows up with a surprise guest, and then Ben is called north to Taos Pueblo for work, most of the holiday plans need a quick makeover.

Ben goes to Taos to offer grief counseling to the community after one of their most respected pueblo dancers collapsed and died during a ceremony. He arrives to find Taoseños in shock, both at the pueblo and within the larger community. Within days the rumor is out: The dancer's death was not a heart attack, and Ben finds himself looking into what might have really happened. Theories and suspects are everywhere, and the Pecos family is trying hard to capture the holiday spirit despite Christmas headwinds.

Thank you for taking the time to read *The Homecoming*. If you enjoyed it, please consider telling your friends or posting a short review. Word of mouth is an author's best friend and is much appreciated.
Thank you,
Connie Shelton

There's more coming!
In the meantime, if you've missed any…
Turn the page to get the links to all of Connie's books.

Books by Connie Shelton

The Charlie Parker Series
Deadly Gamble
Vacations Can Be Murder
Partnerships Can Be Murder
Small Towns Can Be Murder
Memories Can Be Murder
Honeymoons Can Be Murder
Reunions Can Be Murder
Competition Can Be Murder
Balloons Can Be Murder
Obsessions Can Be Murder
Gossip Can Be Murder
Stardom Can Be Murder
Phantoms Can Be Murder
Buried Secrets Can Be Murder
Legends Can Be Murder
Weddings Can Be Murder
Alibis Can Be Murder
Escapes Can Be Murder
Old Bones Can Be Murder
Sweethearts Can Be Murder
Money Can Be Murder
Road Trips Can Be Murder
Cruises Can Be Murder
Deceptions Can Be Murder
Holidays Can Be Murder - a Christmas novella

The Samantha Sweet Series

Sweet Masterpiece
Sweet's Sweets
Sweet Holidays
Sweet Hearts
Bitter Sweet
Sweets Galore
Sweets Begorra
Sweet Payback
Sweet Somethings
Sweets Forgotten
Spooky Sweet
Sticky Sweet
Sweet Magic
Deadly Sweet Dreams
The Ghost of Christmas Sweet
Tricky Sweet
Haunted Sweets
Secret Sweets
Garden Sweets
Spellbound Sweets – a Halloween novella
Thankful Sweets – A Thanksgiving novella
The Woodcarver's Secret – prequel to the series

The Heist Ladies Series

Diamonds Aren't Forever
The Trophy Wife Exchange
Movie Mogul Mama
Homeless in Heaven
Show Me the Money

Children's Books

Daisy and Maisie and the Great Lizard Hunt
Daisy and Maisie and the Lost Kitten

Sign up for Connie Shelton's free mystery
newsletter at www.connieshelton.com
and receive advance information about new
books, along with a chance at prizes, discounts and
other mystery news!

Contact by email: connie@connieshelton.com
Follow Connie Shelton on Twitter, Pinterest and
Facebook